# KILLER GHOST

A CHRISTIE'S FLOWER SHOPPE MYSTERY

PJ PETERSON

Copyright © 2026 by PJ Peterson

All rights reserved.

No part of this book may be reproduced in any form or by any electronic or mechanical means, including information storage and retrieval systems, without written permission from the author, except for the use of brief quotations in a book review.

This is a fictional story. While there a few actual place names, the characters and actions are entirely created from my imagination.

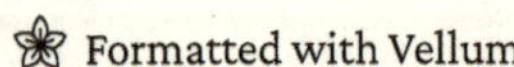 Formatted with Vellum

# DEDICATION

*I'm dedicating this story to **Polly Robinson**, one of the former owners of a mansion set high on the hill behind the high school that I attended many years ago.*

*Polly kindly shared some photos of the home from the time she owned it, as well a few older pictures. It was exquisitely grand with tall ceilings, oak floors, five fireplaces, a dining room with oak beams and leaded windows, and a butler's pantry. It also included maid's quarters and even a safe, in which she found an abstract of the original purchase in 1906. While it has a widow's walk now, it was added later.*

*I wasn't able to tour the house personally, but my friend Marcia Ferrel had been inside and shared a few details. She's the one who planted the seed about writing a ghost story.*

*A disclaimer—the house is not known to be haunted, although a few other homes in my hometown are thought to be, according to local legend.*

# CHAPTER ONE

Christie and Anita secured the last of the deep blue hydrangeas onto the pergola at the edge of the patio and stepped back to admire their work.

"That is absolutely gorgeous," said Anita. "The decorations get more beautiful with every wedding you do. The navy of the blooms and sage greenery and ribbons are a wonderful color combination!"

Christie O'Mara beamed as she felt her face redden. She'd only owned her flower shop for a short two years but felt great pride in continuing the tradition of her grandmother's floral displays. Her long-time friend Anita Sanders helped her with events like weddings and receptions that took place outside the shop itself.

"Thanks, Anita. I'm hoping these colors will create a bit of magical mystery. But the good kind, of course," she added quickly.

Anita cocked her head at her business partner. "Of course. What other kind is there?"

Christie shrugged. "Well, they say this mansion might be haunted."

Anita laughed. "Right. That's exactly the kind of publicity that attracts clients. Like how we offer 'love with every bouquet.' "

Christie had to laugh at that. "Well, we do, of course." And the two friends smiled.

Christie began gathering her tools and leftover ribbons and greenery. "Let's take this stuff to the van. Then we can finish the last bit inside the ballroom."

A few minutes later, the two of them walked through a lavishly decorated arch, then down the aisle as though they were bride and groom. Anita hummed the "Wedding March" as they slowly made their way to the altar, actually a stage for the mansion's ballroom, stopping every few steps so Christie could inspect the floral pew decorations on the aisle chairs.

"Did you notice the photographs along the back wall?" Anita asked when they turned to evaluate the room's decor from the altar. Christie shook her head. "Follow me."

A small collection of ornately framed photographs hung on the long wall that was divided in the center by the entry door. One of them showed a dozen women in Victorian-style gowns dancing with gentlemen in evening dress. A quintet of musicians was tucked into the corner. Another depicted what looked like a birthday party in a dining room.

"Hmm," said Christie, "I wonder where that dining room is or was."

"It's probably part of the banquet hall where the caterers will be working," said Anita.

Christie nodded. "The photos of the ballroom must have been taken at one of those parties Mrs. Lindemann mentioned. She told me this mansion was originally called Langley Manor and that there used to be fancy balls that the locals all attended."

"It looks like it was beautifully decorated. It's too bad this old mansion has a reputation of being haunted, although that can go two ways," said Anita, sighing.

"True. The rumor about it being haunted might repulse some people, but that's exactly the reason Tiffany, the bride for tomorrow's wedding, wanted to use it. She thought it sounded exciting." Christie shivered involuntarily. "Aunt Doris thought it was more weird than exciting. I'm sure I heard her mumbling something about throwing a hex while she was putting those pew decorations together."

Christie's aunt--technically her great-aunt--had worked in the flower shop for her sister, Christie's grandmother, for years before her Grandma Maude passed away and left the shop to Christie. She'd never married and was known as "Aunt Doris" by everyone. She had a halo of frizzy red hair on her head despite her age of seventy-something. Aunt Doris wasn't only a talented flower designer but a matriarch in the community. And she had more than her share of opinions about whatever happened in their small town.

A loud *thunk* sounded through the air. Both young women froze.

"That came from upstairs," said Christie. "We were both upstairs earlier, and there wasn't anything or anyone up there. We'd better see what it was."

"Really? What if it's a ghost?" Anita stood rooted to her spot.

"Oh, come on, Anita. The sound probably just came from something that fell over. I just want to be sure it isn't something we caused by our set-up." They'd been given the keys to the mansion by the owner, Mrs. Lindemann, for their wedding flower decorations and left alone to tend to their displays.

Christie moved quietly to the staircase leading to the second floor, Anita close behind. "I'm going with you," said Anita. "In case you need help."

Christie grinned over her shoulder. "And because you're afraid to stay down here alone."

"Okay, that too."

They crept up the stairs, alert for any other sounds. At the top of the staircase, Christie flipped a light switch in the hallway. They stood still for a moment. Another *thunk* startled them.

"It came from that room," Anita whispered, pointing to the second door on the right. "Maybe someone is in there. You open the door. I'll cover you."

Christie tiptoed to the door and tried the handle. The door opened with a creak. A large, ginger tabby cat sauntered out of the room as though it had been waiting for them. It sniffed Christie's shoe for a moment, then Anita's. It purred loudly as it rubbed its luxurious fur against Anita's leg.

"So you're the culprit! Just what did you knock over?" Christie addressed the cat, grinning.

Anita picked up the purring cat and followed Christie. They quickly searched the room that contained a vanity table and a pile of cardboard boxes. Several chairs leaned against a wall. A lone chair lay on its side near the window, which was ajar about six inches.

"The cat must have tipped over the chair and made that sound," said Christie.

"It makes sense, but why is that window open?" Anita peeked out. "I wouldn't think the owner leaves any of them open between events."

"I doubt the cat opened it, but I'd guess that's how it got in." Christie let the cat jump to the floor.

Anita nodded. “They do climb, so that could be it.”

“Or... maybe it really is a ghost cat, and it can walk through closed doors.” Christie giggled. As she closed the window, a whisper of cold wind brushed her neck. Yet when she looked outside, the nearby tree’s leaves hung still, not fluttering at all.

# CHAPTER TWO

"Did you ask the owner about the kitty?" Anita asked during the drive to Langley Manor the next morning. "I hope she had a logical explanation."

"Mrs. Lindemann thought it might belong to the caretaker. He lives in a small cottage at the back of the property and keeps an eye on the building. Apparently, there have been incidents in the past with people entering the grounds without permission and he escorts them off the property. She said he also keeps the grass mowed and makes simple repairs. One of his most important duties is to be sure everything is ready and in working order for the events she schedules. And he lets the cleaning service in when needed."

"Okay, but why was the cat in the house if the caretaker wasn't there?"

"That's easy." Christie turned to smile at her friend. "It's a mouser and has free run of the house and property. It earns its keep by catching mice."

Anita shivered. "I don't like mice at all."

"We haven't seen any, so the cat must be doing its job."

The graveled parking area was partially filled with cars when Christie and Anita pulled up. The wedding party—bride and groom, best man and maid of honor in dark blue, and six bridesmaids in a lighter shade of blue with escorts—was assembled on the patio for pictures. Two sets of parents hovered nearby, awaiting their cue to be in a photo or two or three.

A young photographer wearing a white shirt, black trousers with suspenders, and a mop of curly, black hair called out orders to the group. "Chins up! You, sir, on the end. Stand a little closer to your neighbor. No, the other neighbor." The mood lightened and the smiles were more relaxed.

Christie whispered to Anita as they got out of the van. "I'm glad Tiffany's mom picked up the corsages and boutonnières earlier this morning for the pictures." She held her hands in prayer position for a second. "It saved me from having to be here an hour earlier."

Anita carried a basket full of nosegays and rose petals for the flower girls, while Christie pulled a utility wagon with two huge vases of flowers through the main entrance. It opened into a grand foyer with a floor that was tiled in large, black and white squares.

They took a right turn toward the kitchen, which functioned as a sort of butler's pantry for events. The caterer had already set up shop with stacks of clear plastic plates, baskets of silverware and napkins in two shades of blue, and tall pitchers of a sparkling, rose-colored beverage ready for the reception that was to follow the wedding.

"Hi, Vivien," Christie said. She'd encountered the popular caterer at other events. "We'll stay out of your way. I just need a little space for the next few minutes or so to finish these bouquets."

"Ooh, I like those!" said Vivien with a squeal. "They're lovely. Those delphiniums are a gorgeous shade of blue. It's light but rich at the same time. And they're beautiful with the white roses."

"Thank you! Okay, Anita. Let's finish these and get them placed in the front of the ballroom where the wedding ceremony will take place."

Task completed, Christie and Anita headed out to the patio where the reception was to follow. They'd decorated the white archway the previous day with white and blue ribbon streamers and a mass of hydrangeas in several shades of blue and white. It was a beautiful entrance to the aisle where Tiffany and Drew would slowly walk on their way to the altar.

Christie took a big breath and clasped her hands against her chest. "It's pretty, isn't it, Anita?' she said as she turned toward her friend.

"Christie!" Jason Princeton called from the parking area and waved his hand. "Wait there a minute. I'll join you." He crossed the 200-foot expanse quickly with his long strides.

Christie couldn't help but smile at the man who had become her best beau. They'd known each other in high school but hadn't dated then. He was six feet tall with dark hair and deep blue eyes. Despite his physique, he hadn't cared much about sports, preferring to read and study. He'd returned to White Castle in southwestern Washington three years before Christie and had opened a law practice. The past two years he had also helped her solve the mysteries that she encountered.

"Hi, Anita. Hey, Christie," he said, nodding. He quickly surveyed the decorated patio with high-top tables scattered about, party lights hanging from the pergola, and a long table set up for the food, which would be set out by the caterer during the wedding ceremony. "Everything looks beautiful out here." He smiled at Christie. "You're quite the genius, you know." He gave her a little squeeze.

"Thanks. Hey, do you want to take a quick tour of Langley Manor before too many people get here for the wedding? It's not supposed to start until four o'clock, so we have a little time to check it out. You've never been here before, have you?"

"Nope. I didn't even know it existed. You can't see it from the road or from downtown."

"Mrs. Lindemann, the owner, said it used to be visible as far away as the highway below because it sits up on this hill where the high school used to be. Unfortunately, all the trees have grown up in the hundred and twenty years since it was built, so you can't see it from any direction anymore."

"Being closed in by its own forest makes it seem more haunt-worthy, I suppose," said Jason.

Christie nudged him in the ribs with her elbow.

Jason cringed as if in pain and cried, "Ouch! *You're* the one who said it might be haunted."

"No. It was the bride, Tiffany, who told me that story. Anyway, let's go check out the mansion. I'll tell you more when we get inside.

"This way," she said, leading Jason and Anita toward the hallway to their left. She stopped at the foot of a stairway like a tour guide might. "There are two ways to get to the second floor. This is the main one, and it goes to the bedrooms. The other one is on the other side of the kitchen, where the caterer is right now. It goes to what used to be the maid's quarters many years ago."

"Someone spent a lot of money on this," said Jason. "I can't even imagine how much it would cost in today's dollars."

"More than I'm making at the flower shop," said Christie wryly. Her golden bob of curls bounced and her green eyes sparkled as though she had been born in Ireland herself.

"Or teaching at White Castle High School," offered Anita. The tall blue-eyed brunette wore her hair in a chin length bob much like she'd worn it in high school, but with a modern flair to the style. She supplemented her meager teacher's salary with landscape designs. Christie helped Anita in her landscaping and, in turn, Anita helped Christie set up events like today for the flower shop.

When they reached the second floor, Christie opened the first door to the right, which had been assigned to the bridesmaids. A hand-painted sign on the door said as much. Clothes and garment bags were strewn around the room. Several makeup trays lay on the top of the vintage vanity dresser near the sole window.

The next door was labeled "Groomsmen." When Christie pushed it open, she did a double-take. The ginger tabby looked up at her from a chair. "Hi, kitty. I really need to have a name for you if we're going to keep meeting like this."

Jason had a quizzical look on his face.

Anita explained that they'd met the cat yesterday in a different room.

"This room, in fact," said Christie, as she opened the door to the second room on the right. She noted that the chair was still upright as they'd left it the day before, but the window was open. "That's funny."

"What's funny?" Jason asked.

"I'm sure we left the window closed when we were here yesterday. We heard a thud from downstairs and came up to check. The cat came out of this room when I opened the door, and we found that the chair had been knocked over. We assumed that the cat had come in through the open window, so I closed it."

"So what?"

"Someone has been in here and opened the window since yesterday," said Christie.

"I repeat... So what?"

Christie shook her head. "Oh, it's probably nothing. Probably the caretaker did it. He gets everything ready for weddings and such, and he would've been up here getting these rooms set up for today."

"Except that it doesn't look like it's being used today," Anita noted.

The sound of music floated through the window from the stairs. "I hear them warming up for the wedding downstairs," said Anita.

Christie checked her watch. "I need to check on some last minute details. Let's head downstairs. We can finish the tour while the rest of them are doing all their toasting and celebrating."

The ginger tabby followed them down the stairs.

# CHAPTER THREE

Christie, Anita, and Jason quietly joined the guests in the ballroom. They found three seats together in the very back row and quickly sat down as the four-piece orchestra began to play the processional music for the ceremony. The groom, Drew Simpson, and his best man stepped into place from the right side of the room.

The six bridesmaids and their escorts followed. The women were gowned in sapphire blue satin dresses complemented by small bouquets of pink ranunculus and white carnations. The groomsmen wore gray tuxedos with blue cummerbunds and boutonnières that matched the color of the attendants' dresses.

Christie recognized the maid of honor, Stephanie, from the consultations at her shop. She was beautiful in a long gown of midnight blue sapphire; her bouquet had been fashioned with soft pink roses and white carnations. Sage green ribbons trailed down the front of the dress.

The tow-headed ring bearer wearing a little boy's white tuxedo and carrying a midnight blue velvet pillow entered next. His five-year-old face was a mask of seriousness as he walked slowly up the aisle, never cracking the least bit of a smile. He almost ran the last few feet to safety in front of the best man.

Next, a pair of adorable five-year-old twins with long, blonde curls dressed in coral dresses tossed their flower petals from baskets adorned with cascading ribbons. One of them walked slowly down the aisle, glancing from right to left, as though she'd done it all her life. The other child stopped every few yards, put her basket down, and twirled before moving again and dropping another handful of flower petals. The audience giggled while the little girls' mother shook her head and shrugged, her face blushing.

The music paused for a moment, then restarted with the first few bars of the "Wedding March." Everyone stood and turned their eyes to the back of the ballroom to see the bride for the first time, escorted by her beaming father.

Tiffany Grant was gorgeous in an ivory satin off-the-shoulder dress which featured a long train. Thousands of tiny pearls adorned the bodice of the dress, the veil's headpiece, and along both sides of the veil itself. She carried an exquisite bouquet of tiny white and pink roses, dark blue "China" roses, and wisps of baby's breath. Christie couldn't help but smile at how pretty it was, proud to have created all the bouquets and flowers for the ceremony. She hoped Grandma Maude was smiling and approving of her work from heaven.

Once the bride was handed to her husband-to-be, everyone was invited to sit down for the wedding rites to begin.

Christie felt her heart twitter a bit when Jason reached over to take her hand. She smiled shyly at him, wondering what he might be thinking. He winked and looked away, a small smile on his lips.

Outside in the darkening June sky, the patio was now resplendent with high-top tables adorned with short vases of blue, coral, and creamy white flowers and sage green ribbons on top of navy tablecloths. Standing near the side door that led into the kitchen, observing without being in the way, Christie, Jason, and Anita admired the finished look.

Vivien and her staff of three young men dressed in black pants, white shirts, and gold vests hustled back and forth with platters of food destined for the buffet table. A local band played loud, popular music for the wedding guests, who numbered about sixty. The nattily dressed group laughed, talked, and mingled as they sipped their drinks while waiting for the bride and groom to emerge after signing their marriage papers.

"Doesn't it seem to be taking longer than usual for Tiffany and Drew to join their guests?" Christie said to Anita. She had to raise her voice to be heard over the music.

Anita flashed a smile. "It just seems longer because we have to hang out until the party is over to reclaim all your vases and baskets."

Christie sighed. "Yeah, I suppose. One of these days, I'll invest in throwaway vases so I don't have to worry about getting them back."

Anita scoffed. "No, you won't. You'll just fuss over how wasteful they are and keep using the ones you have already."

"You know me too well," said Christie with a smile. "I wish I could've talked Mrs. Lindemann into letting me pick them up later, but she insisted that I clean up today right after the wedding. She has something going on here tomorrow, and they need to set up in the morning."

"Bummer."

Christie's eyes wandered across the parking area to a large, grassy field behind the mansion. A beat-up pickup truck drove into view from the left. Christie watched as the truck stopped and a man hopped out. He walked slowly with a visible limp but soon disappeared from view. She moved along the edge of the patio to see if the cottage that Mrs. Lindemann had mentioned was his destination.

The crowd's conversation suddenly hushed, and all eyes turned to the entrance of Langley Manor, where Tiffany and Drew stood for a moment before making their way to the patio. The guests broke into applause and cheered as the newly-married couple picked up two drinks from one of the waiters.

Drew announced, "Let the party begin!" and the band resumed playing raucously.

"I think we can start retrieving my gear now," said Christie. "Everyone is out here, so they won't notice that we're working."

"Works for me," said Jason.

"Me too," agreed Anita.

"Jason, why don't you bring the van around to the front while Anita and I gather the vases and baskets? That'll save a few steps and a little time." Christie tossed her keys to Jason's open hands.

The ballroom was empty, as Christie had guessed it would be. She and Anita quickly picked up the vases of flowers next to the makeshift altar and the now-empty baskets in the kitchen that had held the nosegay favors.

"What about the tabletop flowers outside?" Anita asked as she placed a basket next to the door for loading into the van.

"Tiffany is going to invite the guests to take them home. She paid extra for the vases so she could do that."

"That was a great idea! One less thing to store back at the shop. How did you think of it?"

"I didn't," said Christie. "Aunt Doris thought of it when Tiffany asked about being able to keep some of the decorations afterward. It's a win-win for me."

"There's Jason with the van," said Anita. "Such a gentleman!"

Christie smiled. "Absolutely." She felt lucky to have him as a close friend and confidante. They'd been seeing each other for about two years, but Christie still felt reluctant to actually call him her "boyfriend." She wasn't sure if he felt the same and was almost afraid to ask.

"I just remembered that there are a few props upstairs on the second floor that I didn't use," said Christie. "We can carry them to the van in one trip if all three of us help."

"Let's do it," said Jason, leading the way to the stairs. Christie and Anita caught up with him, and they all gathered the pillars and boxes in the hallway beyond the dressing rooms.

They froze when they heard a blood-curdling scream.

"It came from upstairs," said Christie. "I don't think there's anything up there except the widow's walk."

"Didn't Mrs. Lindemann tell you it was locked?" Anita asked.

"The sound came from this direction," said Jason. He ran toward the other end of the hall, where a set of stairs were partially hidden behind a chimney that rose from the ballroom below. He raced up the wooden stairs with the girls on his heels.

Christie found a light switch and flipped it on. Anita pulled up the rear with the big tabby right behind her.

"Call 911!" Jason yelled from the landing. "She's still breathing."

# CHAPTER FOUR

Christie dialed 911 and gave the dispatcher the basic information. The young woman lying on the floor was unconscious, but she was breathing and had a weak pulse. It appeared that she'd fallen down the stairs from the fourth level, where the widow's walk was located. Her head was torqued at a strange angle from the rest of her body, and Christie feared the worst for her. She was wearing a dress from the Victorian era but otherwise looked like a typical wedding guest. Jason gently placed his jacket over her while reminding the others that they didn't dare try to move any part of her in case her neck was broken.

Christie said, "Anita, I'd like you to stay here with Jason and I'll go downstairs to inform Tiffany and Drew of what's happened."

She hurried downstairs and led the newlyweds away from the crowd before telling them about the injured woman. Tiffany and Drew glanced around the patio as if to see who might be missing.

Tiffany said, “All my bridesmaids are still here, and I don’t remember anyone slipping out. What about you, Drew?”

“Same here.” He took one of Tiffany’s hands. “We’ll see who it is when they bring her down, unless you want to go upstairs before the ambulance arrives.”

Tiffany shook her head violently. “There’ll be a lot of people up there already. I can wait till they bring her downstairs.”

“Okay. Let’s go tell our guests that there’s been an accident and we’ll update them when we know something. I need another drink anyway.”

Tiffany nodded, her makeup tear-streaked. “Okay. We still need to cut the cake and throw the bouquet. I don’t want to let this totally ruin our day.” She looked up at him with a half-smile. He frowned at her but held onto her hands for another moment.

Chief Conway had been invited to the wedding but broke away from the men he’d been chatting with when he noticed Christie talking to the newlyweds. She filled him in on the accident, and he raced up the stairs as ambulance sirens sounded up the driveway and into the yard.

Christie directed the EMTs to the third floor, where they did a quick evaluation of the unfortunate victim and began the process of stabilizing her for transfer to the hospital.

By the time Christie hustled up the stairs, Conway had already noticed the stairs and the unlocked padlock. He called McAvoy to join them at the scene.

“Christie O’Mara,” said Chief Conway. “Well, well, well. We haven’t had enough excitement around here recently, so thank you for giving us something to do other than write speeding tickets.”

“I’m an innocent bystander, I’ll have you know,” Christie replied. “Jason and Anita will vouch for me.”

Detective McAvoy had arrived a moment earlier amid the hubbub. He whipped out his ever-present notepad and pen. "I believe you, Christie. Go ahead and tell me what you know."

Christie, Anita, and Jason each related basically the same story. The only detail that was different was Christie having noticed the man and the truck behind the building. But she was unable to identify any relevance at the moment.

The EMR technician interrupted. "We're going to transport this young lady to the hospital now, Officer, if that's okay with you. She's not going to make it otherwise. It's pretty iffy."

"Of course," said McAvoy. "Let me take a quick photo of her face to help with getting an identification. I'll finish interviews here and follow along later."

As she stood waiting, Christie spotted a piece of paper on the floor where the victim had lain. She picked it up with her fingernails and held it up to read. It was an invitation to the wedding, albeit smudged and creased. She offered it to Detective McAvoy, who opened an evidence bag and labeled it.

"I wonder if she was an invited guest to the wedding," said Christie. "And if she was, why was she up here instead of in the ballroom or on the patio?" She tossed a look to McAvoy. "And was she pushed? Or did she fall? And was she by herself?"

"If this is an official invitation, Tiffany or Drew should know who she is," said Anita.

"Are they the bride and groom?" McAvoy asked Anita.

"Yes. They're about the same age as this young lady. She could've been a classmate or something." Anita chewed on her lip.

McAvoy gestured up the stairs with his thumb. "What's up there? Did you already check?" He looked at Christie when he asked the question.

"That's a widow's walk that Mrs. Lindemann said was locked up so nobody could go up there," she replied.

McAvoy nodded his appreciation. "Who's Mrs. Lindemann?"

"She's the owner of this house."

"I see."

Chief Conway said, "I'll look around here, then go down and start interviewing. McAvoy, why don't you forward that photo to me and then take Miss O'Mara up to that widow's walk and check it out. I'll take Jason and Anita with me. It might be helpful to have another set of eyes and ears for the interviews."

"Sure, Chief."

McAvoy climbed the short flight of stairs to the third level, stopping at the entrance to the widow's walk. "I want to look for any footprints before we look over the rail. Stay here, please." Slightly bent over, he scanned the walkway and took a few photos with his phone. He motioned for Christie to join him. "I see at least two sets of prints here in the dust. There may have been someone else up here with her. Or it's possible they may have been left at another time."

Christie knelt to investigate closer. "The victim was wearing a pair of low-heeled pumps. These prints could definitely belong to the young lady," she said, pointing to one set of footprints in the dust. "She couldn't have worn more than a size six shoe. " She looked up at McAvoy for his reaction. "If someone else was up here with her, do you think it's possible this wasn't a simple accident?"

He jerked his head toward the rail, from where they could see the remnants of the reception below. "I wonder if someone at the party down there saw what was going on up here. Maybe we'll get lucky and get an identification of one or both parties." His face remained flat, as though he didn't believe in that happening.

McAvoy took several more photos of the footprints from different angles, then they both headed back down the ladder-like stairs. The ginger tabby sat in the hallway, its tail flicking slowly back and forth.

# CHAPTER FIVE

Chief Conway was in the ballroom with Tiffany and Drew when Detective McAvoy and Christie came down the stairs. Conway turned when he heard their footsteps.

"Neither the bride nor the groom recognized the young lady," he said as he closed his notepad. "They said they don't know why she had an invitation. As far as they knew, she wasn't dating any of their close friends and wasn't a family member of anyone they knew."

Tiffany and Drew nodded grimly.

"Didn't you hear the scream?" Christie asked.

Drew said, "Not at all. The music was pretty loud and everyone was talking."

Tiffany nodded and took a sip from the almost empty champagne glass in her hand.

Conway said, "That's all the questions I have for the two of you for now."

Drew asked, "Are we free to go yet, Chief? We'd like to go to the airport for our flight."

"Is that okay with you, McAvoy?" Conway asked of his lead detective.

"No, sir. It's not okay," McAvoy replied tersely. He stepped away a few feet and signaled Conway to join him. They turned away from the young couple, who were talking loudly with each other.

"Why is it not okay, McAvoy? They said they didn't know the victim. What else do you want from them?"

"More information, for one thing. We need to know why the padlock was open. According to Christie, the owner said the entrance to the widow's walk is always kept locked. It makes me wonder if there was someone else involved—someone who was up there with our young victim. Besides, they're probably planning to stay in a hotel tonight and flying out tomorrow. I'll see them at the station first thing in the morning, and they can still leave in time for their honeymoon."

Conway took a big breath. "Give me a few minutes to talk to them. I'll see if that will work."

Christie watched as Tiffany angrily put a hand on her hip when Conway told them he needed them to stay in town until morning to help with the investigation.

"What about our honeymoon?" Tiffany wailed. "Drew paid a lot of money for it."

"It's okay, Tiff," said Drew. "Our flight doesn't leave until tomorrow afternoon. I'm sure the police will be done with us in plenty of time." As Tiffany fumed, he turned to Chief Conway. "What time would the good detective like us to be at the station?"

"I'll be there at eight a.m. Is that too early for you?" McAvoy said with a whisper of a smile on his face.

"We'll be there." Drew grabbed Tiffany's hand, and they rejoined their guests on the patio.

When the bride and groom were out of the room, McAvoy

asked the chief, "Did you learn anything more from any of the guests?"

Conway shook his head. "Nothing very enlightening. We couldn't very well ask everybody about the victim's identity yet, but I didn't hear anyone say that they'd seen anything on the widow's walk. Or heard the scream."

Jason said, "I talked to half a dozen guests. None of them saw or heard anything unusual, and they weren't aware of a problem until the ambulance arrived. They were enjoying the music, which was pretty loud, and talking and laughing."

Anita nodded. "That's the same thing I learned, although one young lady told me that she'd heard Drew played around a lot before he met Tiffany, and they hadn't been engaged very long. She wondered if the victim was one of his old girlfriends who had slipped into the crowd."

"We'll check that out," said McAvoy, scribbling a few more words in his notepad.

"It could make sense if that girl was someone he dated before Tiffany," said Christie offhandedly.

"Then why didn't he say so? And why did she have an invitation?" Jason asked.

"She could've gotten the invitation from a mutual friend," Christie suggested. "And if she was a former girlfriend, he probably isn't going to admit it in front of Tiffany."

"I suppose that's a possibility," McAvoy admitted. "We can ask her at the hospital."

Conway asked, "Did you talk to the catering crew already?"

"Not yet. I wanted to catch as many of the guests as possible before they scattered. I figured the caterers would be the last to leave. Besides, I wouldn't have thought one of them would know any of the wedding guests."

"Okay," said the chief. "Why don't you go inside and talk to them so they can leave. I'll get the guest list from the bride's parents in case we have to make a few phone calls tomorrow."

"Got it," replied his detective. "I want to check out something while Christie and her gang are still here. Then I'll head to the hospital."

McAvoy asked Christie to go back up the stairs to the widow's walk. From the patio below, he directed her to stand in the doorway first, then move across the four-foot-wide space to the outside wall while he watched. He was disappointed to discover that he couldn't see her from below unless she was directly against the outside wall and even then, he could barely see her head.

"It appears that someone could quite easily have been up there without being witnessed," said McAvoy once she returned.

"And the music would've easily covered up any sounds from the rooftop," added Anita.

One of the waiters passed by on his way to his car in the parking area. "Excuse me, Officer, but I just remembered that I might have seen something, although I'm not sure it's relevant."

"What is it, young man?" McAvoy flipped his notebook open. "First, what was your name?" He gave the trio a raised brow and nod to the side. The indication was clear: this wasn't their business, and they should step away. They did, but not so far that they couldn't still hear the conversation.

"Oliver, Sir. Oliver Whitman."

"Please tell me what you saw, Oliver."

"Well, I had to go outside to the catering van and get more plates, and I saw someone running across the field over there to a silver car. It just seemed odd. To be running, I mean." He pointed to the grassy area behind the mansion toward the parking area.

"Can you describe him and the car?"

"He was on the thin side, had dark hair, and was wearing jeans and a black jacket. He didn't look like a wedding guest to me, and he wasn't one of our catering staff. Anyway, he got into a silver SUV, but I can't tell you what make. They all look so much like each other nowadays. It was kinda dusty, though, like it hadn't been washed lately. That's all I saw, and then he took off down the driveway."

"What time did that happen?"

"Well, the reception had already started, but I can't tell you the exact time. I'm sorry I didn't look at my watch. I was kinda busy and Vivien, my boss, was yelling for me to hurry."

"That's fine, Oliver. Any other detail? Did you hear the woman scream?"

"No, sir. Not over the music and the noise."

"But you heard your boss yelling?"

"Yeah, but that was when I was still inside and she was standing right next to me."

"Okay. I'll call you if I think of anything else."

"Yes, sir. I gave my number to the other policeman." Oliver pointed to Chief Conway.

McAvoy's phone buzzed in his shirt pocket. "McAvoy. Oh. That's too bad. Thanks for the call. We'll be there in about fifteen minutes." He turned to Christie. "That was the hospital. The young woman died in the ambulance. They're hoping I can tell them who she is... was." He grimaced.

Once Conway and McAvoy had left for the hospital, Jason helped Christie and Anita grab the last of the vases that had been left behind on the tables and the props they'd left upstairs. Conway had already draped yellow Crime Scene tape at the bottom of the stairs off the ballroom, so they carefully put it back in place when they were done.

They watched as a Cadillac Escalade pulled up into the almost empty parking area. Christie guessed it was the crew coming to set up for the event scheduled for the next day. She wondered if it would be canceled, considering that Langley Manor might now be a murder scene.

"I'll buy you ladies a drink at the Silver Spoon Saloon when you get there," said Jason.

"I'd like that," said Christie. "Something seems off here. We can share our thoughts over food and beer."

# CHAPTER SIX

The trio sat at a round table in the corner of the room. Loud music played in the background while several screens silently displayed games of different sports: soccer, basketball, and golf. Jason had ordered a pitcher of beer and a platter of appetizers. In the meantime, the server brought a basket of warm tortilla chips and *queso* dip to enjoy with the cold beer.

"Looks good," said Christie, "but my appetite goes away when death is involved, especially if it was murder."

"We don't know yet that the girl was murdered," cautioned Jason. "It's more likely an accidental death at this point."

"It's hard to believe she was up there all by herself," said Christie. "I wonder if she was with someone—a boyfriend maybe. It looked like there was at least one other set of footprints up there, and they looked more like a guy's shoe."

"I'm not sure I have an appetite either," said Anita. "She was a pretty girl, and her life is gone, just like that."

Christie reached over and placed a hand on Anita's arm.

"The best thing we can do is help Detective McAvoy figure out what happened—as much as he'll let us anyway."

Anita nodded and wiped her sniffly nose.

Christie rummaged in her tote and found the small notebook that she carried around with her. It was handy to jot down notes about flowers that she wanted to use in bouquets, or for reminders of what she needed at the shop when she was going to the wholesale warehouse thirty miles up the freeway from her home and business in White Castle. While she tried to do most of her business in her own cozy little town, where almost everybody knew each other, some things just weren't available.

"I'll start," said Christie. "We have an unidentified female, about twenty-five years old, pretty, wearing a vintage-style dress, and she appeared to have an invitation to the wedding."

"And that young man from the catering service reported seeing a dude running from the building to his car about the same time we heard the scream," said Jason.

"Actually, he didn't say he heard the scream," said Anita, "so we don't know for sure what time that was relative to finding her."

"I saw an older man come from around the side of the house and walk toward the back of the property just before the reception started," said Christie. "He walked with a definite limp. I wonder if he's the caretaker the owner had told me about. She said he lives in a small cottage on the property."

"We need to tell the detective about him," said Anita. "He might know something helpful."

The appetizers arrived with three plates, a bowl of fresh salsa, and a pile of napkins.

"Let's eat while the food is hot," said Jason. "The mystery can wait a few minutes."

Despite their lost appetites, the platter was half empty

when Anita said, "The girl might be a local. Maybe she went to White Castle High School. I could ask around on Monday and see if any of the teachers remember her."

"It would be helpful to have a name," said Jason.

"McAvoy probably has one by now," said Christie. "It can't be that hard to identify her in a community this small."

"*If* she's a local," said Anita. "There are a handful of smaller towns around here that she could be from. Or she could be from farther out of town, like Chehalis."

"I have a thought," said Jason. "That invitation she was holding could very well have her fingerprints on it."

"But she'd have to have fingerprints in the system for that to help," said Christie. "She didn't look like a criminal."

Jason scoffed. "Most criminals look like normal people, you know. But you're right that she'd have to have been fingerprinted in the past."

"Let's back up. What about talking to that Langley Manor caretaker ourselves?" Christie suggested. "Maybe he saw or heard something relevant? We should certainly at least ask about the padlock to the widow's walk. Mrs. Lindemann said it was always locked. And if I saw him, I could confirm that he was the man I saw limping away outside earlier and that would solve that mystery."

"Good idea. It's funny, though, that no one seemed to know her, especially those who sent out the invitations. Even Tiffany and Drew denied knowing who the victim was when Chief Conway asked," said Anita. "But they could've been lying."

"Yes, they were trying to leave for their honeymoon and more questions could've kept them from making their flight." Jason paused. "In fact, we don't know for sure that they were flying out today. Even that could've been a lie."

"True. I'm glad McAvoy told them they had to stay until

tomorrow morning. They can always change their flight. Anyway, the guy leaving in the silver SUV the caterer saw isn't much of a lead. There must have been at least six or seven silver SUVs in that lot," said Christie. "And that was before the wedding had even started."

Anita groaned. "I can see the headlines now: 'Killer Flowers Strike Again!' "

"That's not funny, Anita!" Christie gave her friend a sour look.

Sadly, their flowers had, in some way, been involved in too many crimes in the past, with an overzealous and insensitive reporter pointing that out in print in the past. Publicity was supposed to be a good thing, but Christie cringed at that type. She sighed. That reporter, as one of the few newspaper staff in their small town, would find this incident more newsworthy than the squabbles of the city council or the new automatic doors just installed at the grocery store.

"I don't think they'd go that far this time to connect us to this, but I wouldn't be surprised to see the reporter make mention that my shop supplied the flowers for the wedding."

Christie rolled her eyes. "There's not much else we can do without the name of the victim," she said. "Maybe Detective McAvoy will call later and tell us who she was."

"Officer Newell might have to get involved as well, with Chief Conway going out of town," said Anita.

"Why would that be?" Christie asked. "Are they that busy?"

"Chief Conway will be in Seattle all week for some kind of police training, so they'll be short-handed. Joe, I mean Detective McAvoy, will be functioning as the interim chief as well as doing most of the detective work. Max Newell will be filling in and helping Joe with any investigations." Anita had been out on a few dates with their local detective, but they'd been very cautious about being seen together in White Castle. Tongues tended to wag. But she'd told Christie and Jason, and they nodded at this "insider" information.

"There'll be plenty for both of them to do with this 'accidental death,' if that's what it turns out to be," said Christie.

Jason picked up the last taquito and dipped it in the salsa and then sour cream. "What about the rumor that Langley Manor is haunted? Did you guys see any ghosts while you were decorating?"

Christie said, "Ghosts are invisible, or so I've heard, so I can't verify that we saw one. But we heard some unusual sounds we couldn't explain, and when we snuck upstairs to check them out, the only thing we saw was that orange cat sitting there with a guilty look on its face."

"Are you suggesting it's a 'ghost' cat?" Jason asked with raised brows.

Christie shrugged. "Even when McAvoy and I were the last to leave the widow's walk, the kitty was sitting in the doorway, flicking its tail." She cocked her head as she recalled the scene. "Too bad it couldn't tell us what had happened."

# CHAPTER SEVEN

Sunday morning, Christie stood in her shop, putting away the reusable items from the wedding. As she wedged the last box into the storage room, she wished again that she had more space for such things inside the shop. There was very little extra capacity in the small room at the back, where she kept boxes of vases, gift items, florist tape, and other supplies. She despaired that there wasn't enough room for the larger boxes that contained the miscellany for weddings and receptions. While she would love to have an arch on hand, for example, she was forced to rent one again and again for lack of space to store it if she did own one.

She stepped out the back door of the shop and examined the space where she and her aunt parked their cars. It wasn't large enough to add a storage shed, but maybe her dad could enlarge her storeroom by pushing the back wall out a few feet. She would ask him when she went to her parents' home for dinner that evening as had become her habit on Sundays.

Her phone buzzed in her back pocket as she went back into the shop. The name "McAvoy" lit up the screen. Eager to hear if he'd learned anything more about the young lady who had died the day before, she answered before the second buzz.

"Hey, Detective. What do you have for me today?"

"Hi, Christie. It looks like we have an ID on the girl from the wedding. One of the nurses in the emergency department recognized her. She's from some small town off the freeway going north. I've talked to her parents, and they went to the morgue earlier for positive identification. They confirmed it was their daughter."

"Did they have any idea why she was at the wedding?"

"The dad was clueless, but the mom was pretty sure that she'd been friends with the groom or one of his friends at some point, but it was a while back."

"Okay." She was pleased to know this but realized the detective had been under no obligation to tell her. She asked, "And you're telling me this because..."

"Mrs. Elliott, the mother, said her daughter, Lauren, had been talking with someone recently about maybe crashing a wedding. She didn't know whose it was but considering the circumstances, this may have been the one."

"Did she say if her daughter had dated the groom?" Christie felt her heart race with this new information.

"She wasn't sure about that. They may have just been acquaintances. She was pretty weepy, as you might expect, and I didn't want to push her too hard right away. A distraught mother talking to a uniformed cop can be uncomfortable for her..."

"Would you like for Anita and me to chat with her? Do you think we might get more information from her?"

"Well, I was thinking she just might be inclined to say more to a woman than a male police detective, even if it's not strictly by the book."

"Is Chief Conway going to be okay with that? I know he doesn't like civilians getting involved all that much."

"Officer Newell and I agree that having you talk with her could be helpful. I can deal with the chief."

"Okay. Give me the name and contact information, and we'll do our best. Where does she live? White Castle?"

"No. She's in a little town about thirty miles north of here. Elida. I've never heard of it, not being a local."

Christie couldn't help but giggle over the name. "That's a funny name for a town. It was probably named for someone's mother or grandmother."

"That was my great-aunt's name, I'll have you know," said McAvoy. "Aunt Elida came from good Norwegian stock."

"McAvoy is hardly a Norwegian name," said Christie.

"It was on my mother's side," he replied. "She was the Scandinavian Olsen from Norway and my uncle was the Scotsman. He was my dad's oldest brother."

"I see," said Christie with a nod that McAvoy couldn't see over the phone. "That explains why you're so stubborn at times."

"Said the Irish lass to the Scotsman," he replied. "Back to the subject—like you suggested, I think that you and Anita would be able to get more information from Mrs. Elliott than I was able to glean from her. I'm not real hot on the idea, but I can use the help with Chief Conway out of town."

"Okay. I'll call Anita and see if she's free this afternoon. I love a road trip on a sunny day like this."

An hour later, Christie and Anita were on their way to Elida, a town of about 1000 residents. It had been a logging town, like so many other small communities in rural Washington, until the 1960s. It now depended on summer tourism for survival with an outdoor art gallery of unique sculptures, murals of historical interest on historic buildings, and a small theater that hosted a series of musicals performed by a children's group every year.

The Main Street shops each had an old Western theme, with names like Wild Bill's Men's Clothing, Annie Get Your Gun Shop, and Coyote Joe's Coffee Shop.

Christie smiled at the clever names as she drove down the street.

"Where do we turn, Anita? We have to be pretty close by now. Mrs. Elliott said she usually walked to the post office, and we just passed it."

"The GPS says to turn left in three more blocks onto Maple Street." Anita counted out the streets as they passed Oak and Cypress. "It's the next street, where that maroon Subaru is parked at the corner. Turn left there."

"Got it. What's the house number?"

"It's 313, a yellow house halfway up the second block on the right-hand side. I can see it already."

Christie pulled her car into the empty space in front of the house. The small yard was planted with tired shrubs that badly needed pruning and flower beds that were overgrown with weeds. She could see that the paint needed some touching up as well. It was faded, with areas of bare wood on the west-facing facade. Maybe the homeowner didn't like to do yard work and couldn't afford to have it done either.

She took a big breath and said, "This could be difficult for Mrs. Elliott, but it has to be done. You being the teacher might have a better approach than me. I'm better with numbers." Educated as an accountant, Christie knew that she sometimes came across as cold-hearted unless she was talking about her favorite subject, which happened to be flowers.

Mrs. Elliott met them at the door. "I saw you coming up the sidewalk. These new-fangled doorbell things come in handy. I never answer the door when I see someone that looks like they're trying to sell me something. Those young men from pest control companies are the worst. They just don't take 'no' for an answer." She held the door open for them. "Please do come in and sit down."

Christie led the way into a pleasant living room with a vintage vibe. The sofa and chairs were a medium shade of green and looked tired but were enlivened by colorful pillows with bright floral patterns. She and Anita sat close together on the sofa. They were joined almost immediately by a small, shaggy dog that had been hiding behind one of the chairs. The little black dog, a terrier maybe, sat next to Christie and began licking her arm.

"Missy! You get down from there. The ladies might not like dogs." Mrs. Elliott scooped up the happy dog which wriggled in her arms, trying to get away. "We don't get a lot of company, so she gets real excited with strangers." She set the dog down in front of her, but Missy jumped up into her lap, immediately lay down, and closed her eyes.

"Thank you for seeing us, Mrs. Elliott," said Anita. "I realize this has to be hard for you, losing your daughter and all."

Mrs. Elliott sniffled into a handkerchief that she pulled out of a pocket. Christie noticed her arthritic fingers. "She's not actually my daughter, although I raised her as such. She's my granddaughter. Her mother, my daughter Cynthia, was killed in a car accident when Lauren was only two years old. Harvey and I have been her 'parents' since then. I'm sorry he couldn't be here, but he's playing golf with his buddies."

"That's all right. We didn't give you much notice that we were coming. Now, we didn't get any information about your daughter—granddaughter— from the detective who called you," said Christie, "except her name. Can you tell us a little more about her, like her age and maybe some friends' names?"

"Well, Lauren had just turned twenty-three last week and came home all excited on Friday, I think it was, a week ago about landing a job at the bank downtown. She wasn't a great student but managed to get an associate's degree in basic bookkeeping at Cascade Community College after four years of part-time school. We were real proud of her because she'd always been so shy. We hoped this new job would give her an opportunity to make some friends." Mrs. Elliott looked up at the ceiling, sighing.

"Can you tell me what you told the detective about her maybe going to a wedding?" Anita asked gently.

"It sounded like her boyfriend was inviting her to one of his friend's wedding, but Lauren didn't really want to go. She said she might see too many of her old classmates."

"Why would that be a problem?" asked Anita. "I'm a high school teacher, and it seems like most girls are excited about seeing their friends."

"Lauren wasn't exactly like most girls. She was overly sensitive and always very shy, but so was I when I was young. She didn't like being in crowds and didn't have but one close girlfriend. She was quiet and loved animals. When she was little, she wanted to bring home every stray kitty or bunny or puppy she saw."

Mrs. Elliott blew her nose using the scrunched-up handkerchief in her hand. "I worried about her being able to hold a job when she got out of school because she was so introverted. She didn't like school very much because she said everyone treated her like she wasn't there. It was almost like she was invisible when she was right in front of you. Not that she wanted attention at all, of course, but no one wants to be invisible either. That's why I was so happy that she finished her degree and landed a job. I thought it was the beginning of a new life for her." Tears flowed down her face and she sniffled again.

Anita nodded, her mouth set in a sympathetic frown. "I understand. Can you tell me anything about this boyfriend of hers?"

Mrs. Elliott's face darkened. "We didn't much like him. He had long hair that always seemed greasy and wore his jeans too low. I wondered if he used marijuana, but Lauren wouldn't listen to me when I told her she could do better. She just clammed up."

"Do you know his name?"

"His name was Adam something. He's not from Elida, so I'm not sure where Lauren met him."

"Would the girlfriend that you mentioned know anything, do you think?"

"Maybe. I've got her name and number in the kitchen." Mrs. Elliott rose with a groan from the wingback chair. "Would you like some tea or coffee as long as I'm up? I should have offered you something earlier."

"Thank you, but we don't want to keep you," said Christie.

Once their hostess was out of earshot, Christie said quietly, "Lauren sounds like a loner."

"From what her grandmother described, she may have just been happy that any guy paid attention to her."

Mrs. Elliott emerged with a yellow sticky note in her hand. "Her name is Jazmine Emerson. I've met her a few times. She seems nice. She and Lauren met at community college, if I remember correctly."

"Has she called you since Lauren died?" Christie asked.

Mrs. Elliott frowned. "No, but it just happened yesterday, so she wouldn't know. I better call her after you leave."

Christie said, "I just thought of something else that might

be helpful. Could we have a look at Lauren's bedroom? It would give us a better sense of who she was and might help the detective solve her death."

"What do you mean by that? Didn't she just fall down those stairs?"

"That's what it looks like, but the question is why was she up there in the first place," said Christie.

"Up where?"

Christie and Anita looked at each other before Christie answered. "She apparently fell down the stairs from the widow's walk to the next floor down."

"But that doesn't make any sense," said Mrs. Elliott. "She told me the wedding was at the Lutheran church. There's no 'widow's walk' there."

# CHAPTER EIGHT

Mrs. Elliott led the way upstairs to Lauren's bedroom. With her hand on the doorknob, she said, "I haven't touched anything in here. I just can't go in there yet." She sniffled again and hurried back downstairs.

Christie opened the door, and they both peered inside.

Anita said, "Everything is neat and orderly. I'm sure my bedroom was never this neat when I was young."

"Lauren's not a teenager anymore," replied Christie. "That could be the difference."

Anita opened the closet door and saw that the clothes were hung both by categories—tops, skirts, pants, dresses—and colors, going from white on the left end to black on the other end of the rod. "I'd say she had a touch of obsessive compulsiveness, at the very least."

Christie peeked in and took note of the orderly closet. "I'd agree with that." She walked around the neatly made twin-size bed with its coordinating comforter and pillow shams in shades of blue. The small wooden desk next to the narrow window was covered with stickie notes. A laptop sat in the middle. Christie asked, "Do you think I should try to open it?"

"I'm sure Mrs. Elliott would agree, but I can ask for you."

Anita stepped out of the room and found Lauren's grandmother in the kitchen. "Would it be okay if we looked at Lauren's laptop? It's on her desk, and it might give us a clue as to what she was up to."

Mrs. Elliott nodded, her lips set in a straight line. "Go ahead. It can't hurt."

"Thanks."

Anita opened the cover of the laptop computer and touched the tab to open it. "What do you think her password might be?" she asked Christie.

Christie opened the single desk drawer. "If she's anything like me, she'll have it on a piece of paper right here at her fingertips. I had to change mine all the time when I tried to open my business account from home because I couldn't remember what I used for the special character. I finally got smart and wrote it down and keep it in my kitchen desk drawer." She rummaged through the miscellany for a moment before finding a small slip of paper taped to the front inside of the drawer. "Aha! Try this." She held the paper out for Anita to see.

"The last password on the list is Adamisdead##," she read out loud. "Hmm. Maybe she and Adam weren't on such great terms after all. She seems to have changed her password recently from 'IlikeAdam21#.'" Anita keyed it in while repeating the code out loud, letter by letter. "Okay, Christie. That worked." She scrolled through the emails and messages, then through the photo gallery. "I see a lot of texts from JZMN, which I would guess is shorthand for her friend Jazmine."

"Anything interesting? Is there any talk about a wedding?"

"Not so far. There are a handful of texts from ADAM12, but they look like instructions related to a lock of some kind."

"A lock?" Christie asked. "Does he say where it is?"

"No, but he ends with telling her to be ready at ten to pick her up."

"What day?"

"This is dated day before yesterday."

"The day before Tiffany and Drew's wedding," said Christie. "It's got to be related to that. McAvoy is going to want to know about this. Let's ask if we can take Lauren's laptop to the detective. I'll take some pictures of the room for him while we're here."

Anita scrolled through a few more photos. "There are several pictures on here that might be Lauren and Adam. The girl is definitely Lauren. Uh-oh. Here's one of Drew."

"Is he with Lauren?"

"She's not in the picture. But I suppose she could've been taking it."

"I have an idea. Go ahead and forward them to me, and I can share them with McAvoy," said Christie. "At least he'll know what Adam looks like."

"Do you see any interesting emails or other texts?"

"I'm looking. I see a few emails from a bank, which are probably related to that new job." Anita scrolled some more. "Nothing helpful here in the rest of these emails going back to January. I'll check her search history."

She was quiet for a minute or two. "Bingo! This might be something."

"What is it?" Christie leaned over her friend's shoulder.

"She's been searching for a birth certificate." Anita looked at Christie. "Her own."

"What? Why would she do that?" Christie pursed her lips in thought. "Wouldn't Mrs. Elliott have one? She would've had to register her for school and all that, and I know they require proof of birth date and all that nowadays."

"She was also looking through local newspaper archives from about twenty years ago."

"That would be around the time her mother died," said Christie. "Can you tell what keywords she was using?"

"Cynthia Elliott, her mother's name."

Christie sat on the edge of the bed while Anita took care of shutting down the computer. "Let's chat with Mrs. Elliott for a few minutes before we leave."

Mrs. Elliott was sitting on the sofa with the dog once again on her lap. "Did you find anything useful?"

"I'm not sure," said Christie. "Do you know why she would be searching for her birth certificate and for details about her mother's death?"

Mrs. Elliott's hands shook, and she took a big breath. "Oh. That." She looked at the ceiling and sighed. "Cynthia never told me who Lauren's father was before she died. I know she didn't name anyone on the birth certificate, but she wasn't dating anyone steady either. I always assumed it must have been a one-night stand or something like that. She was living in Olympia at the time, so I didn't see her regularly."

"Do you have a copy of it?" asked Christie. "And what about the accident? You said her mother died in a car accident. Was there another person in the car?"

"I saved the newspaper articles about that terrible day. I'll get them for you if you have another minute."

"Of course."

Christie took photos of the three articles that Mrs. Elliott had carefully pasted into an old-fashioned scrapbook and of the birth certificate.

"Thank you, Mrs. Elliott. This will save a lot of time not having to scroll through the newspaper archives."

Twenty minutes later, with the laptop in a plastic bag and a copy of the birth certificate and Jazmine's phone number in hand, Christie and Anita thanked Mrs. Elliott and left.

Christie scowled while she started the engine. "Why would Lauren lie about going to a wedding at the Lutheran church? Did she not want her mother to know she was going to the mansion?"

"Maybe Lauren didn't know where she was really going," said Anita. "What if Adam told her a lie in the first place?"

"I just thought of something. What if Adam knew about Drew and Tiffany's wedding and Lauren didn't, and he was going to surprise her by taking her there?"

"Some surprise," said Anita. "Especially if she really did know Drew from the past, like maybe dating him or something."

"Or maybe he could've been trying to get back into her good graces by inviting her to a fake wedding and then did a bait and switch move on her."

"If that's the case, I might wish him dead too," said Anita.

Christie dialed Jazmine's phone number from the car. She heard a cheerful voice say, "Can't talk now. Leave a message." She left her name and phone number but decided not to say anything about Lauren. She didn't want to forewarn Jazmine in any way in case the news about Lauren's death was new to her.

"I suppose we can wait and see if Jazmine calls back before we tell Detective McAvoy what we learned about Lauren today," said Christie as she started the car. "I'm hungry. What about grabbing some lunch downtown? I saw a diner on Main Street. I'll buy."

Eva's Diner was a typical fifties' kind of place, with silver-legged tables with red Formica surfaces, matching chairs with red vinyl seats, and to top it off, vintage jukeboxes at each table. Life-size images of Elvis and Marilyn Monroe graced the walls.

The waitress wore a pink apron over a white blouse and poodle skirt.

"Sorry the jukebox doesn't work anymore," she said with a half-smile as she laid two menus and sets of silverware wrapped in napkins on the table. "But the food's really good, especially the burgers. Can I bring you something to drink?"

Both women asked for iced tea.

"This is straight out of Hollywood," said Christie. "I didn't know there were any of these places left." Christie had seen the old movie *Grease* and imagined the diner could have been from that era.

"It's like the old soda shop in my dad's hometown," said Anita. "We went there once when we were kids. I remember that they still made malted sodas, and we got to sit at the counter with those high stools. I was only ten or so and my feet didn't touch the floor, and I felt really glamorous sitting there drinking a milkshake out of a tall glass with a straw."

"Did you think you'd be discovered by a movie producer like in the old Hollywood days?" Christie asked with a giggle.

Anita replied, "Of course! Didn't we all have that fantasy when we were kids?"

"Back to the reason we're here," said Christie. "I hope we get something helpful from Lauren's friend. Especially the last name of this boyfriend."

"You're going to let McAvoy handle it, I hope," said Anita. "Once we get a name, that is."

"Don't I always?" said Christie with a grin. "By the way, what's the latest with Detective McAvoy? I mean, Joe?"

Anita's face reddened. She and McAvoy had been dating for a few months. She'd admitted earlier that the first few dates were very awkward and she felt like she did all the talking. Eventually, he opened up more and seemed more comfortable in a one-on-one setting.

"He's really very shy, which made it hard for him when he first became a policeman, he told me. He had to put on this stern exterior to talk to people, especially the suspects. He said he did some training at the academy, where he practiced his skills at interrogation with 'pretend' criminals, and it helped a lot to toughen him up or at least to appear that way."

"When is he going to agree to a double-date with Jason and me?"

"Soon, I'm sure. Oh, there's our food. No more questions."

Christie's phone buzzed on the table. "That's Jazmine's number." She put on a bright smile and pressed the green icon. "Hi, this is Christie O'Mara. Is this Jazmine?"

# CHAPTER NINE

"Yes. You left a message to call, but you didn't tell me why."

"First, thank you for calling back. It's about your friend Lauren. Lauren Elliott."

"I just found out that she died yesterday," said Jazmine. "Is that why you called me?"

"Not entirely, but partly," said Christie. "I saw her at the manor after she fell, but I wanted to know about her boyfriend Adam. Do you have a last name for him?"

"Adam's a real jerk, in my opinion. I don't know his last name for sure. Something like Longsword or Longworth. Anyway, he has all these grandiose ideas about making a whole lot of money by getting famous on one of those blog programs and having thousands of subscribers. Ha!"

"Do you know what kind of program he planned to do to get famous?" Christie asked with skepticism.

"It's really stupid, but he thinks that a lot of people would listen to blogs about haunted places, you know, like that mansion up on the hill behind the condos in White Castle. He talked to some old guy about other places around there too. Places you wouldn't suspect, he says."

"Like, what places would those be?" asked Christie, curious.

"Do you know that old house on Cedar Street that was turned into a bed and breakfast last year?"

"Yes. It used to belong to a spinster that my grandmother knew about when she was a young woman. What about it?"

"Well, Adam says that the old lady died there and she wasn't found for days and days, so she was pretty far gone. He said she left a note on the table that the ghosts in the house had been bothering her more and more and were trying to make her leave but she refused. Some people say she was poisoned by the ghosts."

Christie scoffed. "And you believe all this?"

Jazmine said, "Adam says he has proof."

"Do you think you could get Adam to meet with us sometime? I'd love to hear about his ghosts." Christie held up crossed fingers for Anita's benefit.

"I'll try," said Jazmine. "I've got his number somewhere because Lauren gave it to me a while back. He might not know that Lauren died, so I'll tell him that too. I'll call you back later after I talk to him."

"Perfect. Thank you, Jazmine."

Christie shook her head in disbelief as she pocketed her cell phone. She wondered what Jazmine's comment about proof of ghosts meant. She debriefed Jazmine's end of the conversation while nibbling on her burger, which wasn't quite as appealing as it had been when it was hot.

"Ghosts. Hmm." Anita raised a brow while she licked a finger. "That was delicious," she pronounced. She'd been devouring her food while Christie talked on the phone.

"Yeah, ghosts. Wait till I tell McAvoy," Christie said with a grin. "He'll wonder what I've been smoking."

"He knows you don't smoke."

"He may wonder if I've started." She ate a few more bites.

"I'm curious what the caretaker, whatever his name is, knows about the ghost stories about Langley Manor."

"That's a great idea, Anita." Christie checked the time. "We still have time this afternoon."

Back in White Castle, half an hour later, Christie and Anita pulled up to the iron gates at the entrance of the manor's driveway.

Christie punched in the code that she'd been given by Mrs. Lindemann, hoping that it wasn't one of those that changed automatically once the event was done. When she'd called Mrs. Lindemann to ask if they could talk to the groundskeeper, Christie had forgotten to ask about the key code changing. Thankfully, the massive gate with its huge, rusted lions opened, creaking loudly as it did so. She took that as a good sign, as in giving permission for her to do more snooping.

There were no cars in front of the main building. The graveled parking lot was empty. The commercial-sized waste containers near the kitchen had been emptied since the day before. Two of the lids hadn't closed completely, creating a look somewhat like a beret on top of a gigantic green ice cream cone. There was no yellow tape anywhere to be seen.

"It doesn't look like a murder scene at all," said Christie.

"I guess Conway and McAvoy felt they got everything they'd need yesterday," said Anita. "Joe told me that Mrs. Lindemann was quite unhappy that she might have to cancel the event that was scheduled here for today, so she was relieved when the chief told her they were finished."

"It looks like she canceled it after all. I don't see any evidence of anything being set up."

"No, the man who had reserved the place decided to reschedule for another day. He was worried about bad karma, or so he'd told Mrs. Lindemann."

"With a death on the widow's walk, it's got more than bad karma," said Christie. "I'm going to drive around to the caretaker's home in back. Mrs. Lindemann said it had been the living quarters for the gardeners in the early days. The maid who worked here for the original owners lived in the house on the third floor where we found Lauren." She shuddered involuntarily.

Anita asked, "I thought the maid lived on the second floor, where the back stairs go."

"I'm pretty sure Mrs. Lindemann said third floor, but I could be wrong."

"It probably doesn't matter. Anyway, did you ever get a name for the caretaker?"

"Yeah. I finally remembered to ask when I called for permission to talk to him. His name is Larry Flanagan, but Mrs. Lindemann said everyone calls him 'Slim.' "

Christie pulled up in front of the small cottage which had been painted white with dark green trim—a miniature version of the manor, she thought to herself, although the floor plan would be quite different.

"Here we go," she said as she got out of her car. "I'll start with the questions, but you can jump in any time you think of something."

"Deal," said Anita.

They walked up the short sidewalk from the gravel parking area to the door. Christie noticed that the building needed repainting as she got closer. The scraggly shrubs weren't much better looking than the cottage. She knocked on the door using the brass rapper with a lion's head on it.

She heard footsteps approaching from behind her, and jumped.

"Are you looking for me?" asked the scrawny man who appeared from the other side of the cottage. "I don't do the bookings, if that's why you're here. You'll have to call the owner." He turned to leave.

"Mr. Flanagan? Do you have a minute?" Christie said before he could disappear. "Mrs. Lindemann said it was okay to ask you some questions."

He turned back to face Christie, a look of annoyance painted across his dark face. "My name's Slim. What's this about? What kind of questions?"

Christie smiled and said, "I was wondering if you saw a young man leave in a big hurry from the wedding reception that was here on Saturday."

"Why would you need to know something like that?"

"I'm so sorry," said Christie. "I should introduce myself. I'm Christie O'Mara, and this is my friend Anita Sanders. I own the flower shop in White Castle. We decorated the manor and patio for the wedding and reception on Saturday."

"That doesn't explain why you need to know about a young man."

"Did you know that a young lady died that day?"

"Heard from the boss lady. She was pretty unhappy about someone dying here and all. Had to cancel a big revival that the preacher was going to have."

"A revival? Here in White Castle?"

"That's all I know." Slim shrugged one bony shoulder. "Now, why do you need to know about a young man?"

"Well, we're helping the police try to find out what

happened. And one of the catering staff said he saw a young man leaving very quickly about the time the victim was found. Maybe it's nothing, but Detective McAvoy would like to interview him. Did you see him?"

"Can't say that I could have because I wasn't here. I left around noon after I set everything up and didn't come back until about three forty-five, just before the wedding started." He stood with his legs apart, arms across his chest, like he was daring her to challenge him.

Christie almost blurted out that she'd seen him, but asked instead, "Is there someone else you might have seen walking around to the back of the house before the wedding?"

"Might have been someone from the catering crew, I suppose. Gone out for a smoke, maybe. Boss lady doesn't let anyone smoke near the main entrance or kitchen."

Christie nodded. "I guess it could've been one of them."

"Or maybe one of the guests. People like to snoop around here when they see this place for the first time."

"And why is that?"

"There's stories around town about how there used to be big parties up here, you know, when it was new. But that was a long time ago. Now it's almost forgotten about except by the ghost hunters and the occasional wedding or fancy shindig."

Anita nudged Christie in the ribs just as Christie started to say something else and said, "We've heard that the house, I mean Langley Manor, is haunted. Do you know much about that? Is that why the ghost hunters come around?"

He scoffed. "They try to get in, but the gate's almost always locked. Sometimes they've waited at the gate and try to drive in when another car is going in or out. I have to chase them off."

"But is the house haunted?" Anita asked again.

Slim heaved a big sigh. "I suppose I can tell you since you

seem to have heard about it already. About twenty-five years ago, a young girl fell from the widow's walk and died. That's why it got boarded up by the owners back then."

"I suppose it was an accident," said Christie.

"I don't suppose any such thing myself," said Slim. "Rumor was that the young lady was there with her boyfriend. Some people thought he pushed her—maybe on purpose, or maybe not. But he disappeared and was never caught or charged. It might be that her ghost is still here, waiting for the murderer to be brought to justice."

Christie felt her skin chill. "Do you know her name?"

"Sure do. Debra Ellen. She was my niece."

# CHAPTER TEN

"Is that why you're here, because of your niece?" Christie felt an urge to give the man a hug but restrained herself.

"Yes, and because my sister, her mother—her name was Dotty Lewis—asked me to keep looking for the man who was responsible. Dotty died a few years later of a broken heart, in my opinion. Her husband died a few years after that—drank himself to death, I figure. Anyway, Dotty somehow thought that if she wished hard enough, Debra would be alive and it would all have been nothing but a bad dream."

He shook his head. "So when the family who had lived here at the time of the accident sold the place to Mrs. Lindemann, I offered to be the caretaker." He shrugged. "It kinda makes me feel like I'm close to my niece. At the same time, I've always thought the murderer might come back. I'm sure I'd somehow recognize him if he did. And I'd call the police right away if I saw him."

"Do you know who the former owners were?" Christie asked.

"The last name was Donaldson. Charles Donaldson, I believe, was the husband's name. The wife was Sarah. They moved up north after they sold the house, but I don't know any more than that."

"What about the boyfriend?" Anita asked, already thinking of the last names of her students.

"That was a fuzzy detail during the investigation. My sister didn't know any boy Debra was seeing. And the Donaldsons were certain it wasn't one of their own sons. They were quick to name several other friends of their boys who had often spent time at the house. The Donaldsons didn't recognize the young woman, or claimed they didn't. It was never proven one way or the other. I'm pretty sure the police would've interviewed all those young men."

Christie and Anita looked at each other, recalling their first murder case, which had happened several decades before it came to light again and was finally solved.

Christie asked, "Do you have a gut feeling about who the killer was? Do you think it was one of the sons of the household?"

"I'm not sure. I always wondered if it might even be their father, but again, I have no proof or evidence." Slim blew his nose on a dirty handkerchief that he pulled out from a hip pocket. "The 'boyfriend' seemed to be a figment of somebody's imagination. No one could come up with a name, and of course Debra Ellen was dead and couldn't tell us anything. Dotty said there was no regular boyfriend at the time."

"If it was a murder," said Christie, "and it sounds suspicious to me that it was, it might still be an open case. Would you mind if we looked into it a little more?"

Anita shot a glance at her friend, clearly wondering if she'd lost her mind.

Slim shook his head. "Not at all. If you can find the

murderer, Debra Ellen wouldn't have to stay at the mansion any longer. She could move on and join her mother and her father in heaven."

~

ONCE THEY WERE BACK in Christie's car, Anita said, "Are you crazy? Are you really going to try to investigate this one your own?"

"Of course not," said Christie. "I bet Jason would be willing to do some research for me."

"You mean his private investigator, Ben, when you say Jason, I expect. What if he's too busy or says 'No' this time?"

Christie raised a shoulder. "I'll ask Aunt Doris first. She has a memory like an iron fist. She can recall details about an incident that everyone else has totally forgotten!"

Anita sighed, slightly warming to the idea. "True. I've witnessed that talent myself. Do you know if the detective has talked with Jason again about Lauren's death?"

"He hasn't said, so this gives me a reason to ask him about that. What if they're connected?"

"What if what's connected? The two deaths? I don't understand your thinking, Christie. Debra Ellen died twenty-five years ago."

"I can't explain it, but I'm guessing there's something that ties these two accidental deaths together."

"Maybe it's the house itself," suggested Anita. "I mean, the location is the same. And they both involve an unidentified man who may have been on the scene."

"True, but I think we need to look for something else." Christie turned to look at Anita. "Do you understand what I mean?"

"Not really. I don't get those flashes of extrasensory perception that you seem to experience now and then."

Christie sighed. "And I wish I didn't, because I won't be able to let this go until justice has been done. I'll ask Jason about it when I see him later."

CHRISTIE CALLED Joe McAvoy as soon as she got home to tell him about her conversation with Mrs. Elliott, Jazmine, and the caretaker. He chastised her when she confessed that she'd gone beyond what he'd originally asked her to do, but he eventually agreed that talking with Jazmine had been a smart move. Christie had explained that she felt time was of the essence and wanted to get to Jazmine before there was too much social media activity about Lauren's death.

"That's good information about Mr. Flanagan living on the premises, but I don't see that it relates to the current death, Christie."

"I'm not sure it does either," she replied, "but it's quite ironic that two young women died under similar circumstances at the same place."

"It could be simple coincidence and totally unrelated to our current young victim."

"Yes, of course," Christie acquiesced. "But I think you should talk with the caretaker yourself and see what you think after hearing his story. You'll probably get more information than I did. There might even be something in the old newspapers about it that you can check for yourself. Or maybe it's an old cold case sitting in one of those file cabinets at your office."

She heard a loud sigh through the phone. "I don't want to spend time on an old case while working on this one, young lady, but thank you for your help. Let me and Officer Newell handle it from here. I'll pick up Lauren's laptop at your shop in the morning."

# CHAPTER ELEVEN

Having become a regular "date" on Sunday evenings, Jason stopped by Christie's house at five to pick her up for dinner at the O'Maras' home. It had taken Christie's mother, Maureen, many months to convince her daughter to invite Jason to join them for Sunday dinner the first time. Now they joined the older O'Maras every two or three Sundays. Jason enjoyed Maureen's cooking and discussing sports and local politics with her dad, Thomas, while Christie helped her mom with meal preparations.

"Aunt Doris mentioned that the wedding she helped you with was at the old mansion up behind those condos on the hill. Isn't that abandoned?"

"I'm not sure if that's the correct term, Mom. It's definitely not occupied, unless you count the orange cat we found in the building. A woman who lives out of town, Norma Lindemann, owns it now and rents it out for events like weddings and other ceremonies. It's run down from its glory days, but you can still see how grand it must have been when it was built a hundred years ago."

"I remember that some of the high school boys used to sneak up there to smoke when I was in school. It was off limits, of course, and it was inhabited at the time, but that didn't stop them from going through the fence behind the school property to avoid getting caught."

"But the mansion isn't anywhere near the high school, Mom. That doesn't make sense."

"I'm talking about the old school, the one that got torn down in the nineties after they built the new one where you and your classmates went. The boys went through a gap in the fence, or so I've heard."

"Oh. I really never thought about there being a different school building back when you were in school, even though I guess you've mentioned it once or twice. You said it had been built during the Depression, I think."

"That's correct. It was on the hill where those new condos are now."

Christie furrowed her brow. "That makes sense. Those fir and pine trees would've hidden anything going on at the mansion now."

"There were always trees up there, but there are a lot more of them now, and they're taller. When I was younger, you could still see the mansion just beyond the high school from the main road."

"It's not visible from the road anymore," said Christie. "I looked for it when I was coming into town from Elida. It's as if it was never there."

~

JASON AND CHRISTIE lounged on the sofa in Christie's living room after dinner, enjoying a second glass of wine without parental interference. Her little black cat, Stormy, settled herself squarely on Jason's lap and purred blissfully.

"Anita and I went up the road to Elida to meet Lauren's mom and one of her friends today."

"Who's Lauren?" Jason asked. "And where's Elida?"

"Oh, I haven't had a chance to tell you what I've learned about the girl who died after we found her at the wedding Saturday. Her name is Lauren Elliott, and she's from Elida. It's one of those old logging towns off Highway 12 going up to Mt. Rainier. Detective McAvoy called me earlier today and agreed to let me visit her mother and find out more about her daughter."

"And Anita went with you?"

"Yes, and I'm glad she was there. She asked some questions I wouldn't have thought of. Anyway, Mrs. Elliott is really her grandmother, but she raised Lauren since she was a toddler. Her parents, or at least her mother, had died in a car accident. Anyway, she was surprised to find out that Lauren fell from a widow's walk because the wedding she was supposedly going to was at the Lutheran church, not Langley Manor." Christie added the other details they'd uncovered when Jason, being the attorney he was, asked for more information.

"This so-called boyfriend seems to fit the description of the guy who was running off at the mansion," he commented. "Did you get a name?"

"When we talked to Lauren's friend Jazmine, we got a little more information. His name is Adam, last name uncertain, but that's all we got."

"Have you talked to McAvoy yet since your interview?"

"I almost forgot to but Anita reminded me, so I called him just before you came over to pick me up. He wasn't impressed about the earlier death at the mansion." Christie filled him in with more of the caretaker's story.

"I can look into it if you want me to. Ben gets a kick out of this kind of research."

"Oh, thank you, Jason. I was hoping you'd offer your private investigator's services. McAvoy wasn't even willing to look into the old case files at the police station to see if this one was there."

"Consider it done. Maybe Ben will find something interesting, even if it's not connected." He gave her hand a quick squeeze. "Now, who do you have on your suspect list for Lauren's death? I'm sure you've already started one."

"You know me too well," she replied with a giggle. "The most obvious person of interest would be the guy seen running to the silver SUV, of which there are a million around here. His description could fit the boyfriend. I thought of the caretaker, but I watched him limp across the grounds during the reception, and I don't think he could've pushed her and gotten down those stairs fast enough for me to see him only a few minutes later."

"Stranger things have happened," said Jason. "He could be faking the limp, you know."

"Spoken just like a lawyer. Anyway, it occurred to me that it could've been one of the men from the wedding party. McAvoy is going to have to interview each of them to see if there's a connection. I suppose even the young man who worked for the caterer could've been giving false information to deflect blame from himself or one of the other catering staff."

"Of course McAvoy will be working from the same information as you."

"Mom was telling me about how there used to be a high school on the hill in front of Langley Manor, where those condos are now. It was torn down years ago, but I wonder if someone came through the fence in the woods and was waiting for Lauren. Maybe someone knew about it from their mom or dad. That would explain someone running in that direction."

"Okay, but why was Lauren there in the first place? Are you thinking *she* might have snuck in through the fence? I thought you were thinking she came with the boyfriend that her mom mentioned. And that he could be the guy who took off."

"Hmm... There are too many angles here. I think I'll call Jazmine again. She may have talked to Adam by now. And I'll check Facebook for a friend of Lauren's named Adam."

# CHAPTER TWELVE

Christie rushed in through the back door later than usual. Aunt Doris looked at her over the top of her half-glasses.

"What's this I hear about a girl dying at the mansion over the weekend?"

Christie hung up her coat and lifted her shop cat, Stormy, to her observation post above the order desk. "And how did you hear about that already? The newspaper doesn't come out till Friday."

"The groom's aunt talked about it at hospitality at church yesterday. She was pretty unhappy that someone was allowed to go up to that widow's walk. And she wondered why it wasn't padlocked so no one could go up there. She also said that the detective forced the newlyweds to wait an extra day before they could leave on their honeymoon."

Christie sighed and logged onto the computer so she could check her emails for new orders that might have come in over the weekend.—and to give herself a moment to think about a proper response.

"The bride had been assured that there was a padlock on the access door to the fourth floor so no one could go up there."

"Did you check the padlock yourself?"

"Auntie, I didn't have any reason to go upstairs in the first place. And it wasn't my responsibility to make sure it was locked. I was only there for the flowers."

"I understand that, but it's going to look bad when the news hits the street that your flowers were at another event where someone died."

"I know. And I don't know what I can do about that, except hope Detective McAvoy figures out how it happened and if someone was responsible and solves the case quickly." Christie printed the new orders and walked to the front door to unlock it for business.

Doris scoffed. "The aunt said the death was accidental—that the girl fell, or something. Why is McAvoy making such a big deal out of it?"

"I can't tell you everything, Aunt Doris, but he has to talk to a lot of people to be sure it *was* an accident, including Tiffany and Drew. They weren't going to leave for the honeymoon until late on Sunday anyway, so no harm done there."

"I don't suppose you're going to help him again, are you?"

Christie, along with Anita and Jason, had helped the detective solve some cases already, including one that involved a murder that had occurred decades earlier. She avoided answering the question and walked back to the flower room, printed orders in hand, and placed them at the bottom of the short stack in front of her aunt. After grabbing an apron, she selected the topmost order to work on.

"Hmm. This bouquet is for the parents of the bride. Do you think it would be okay to create it using the colors from the wedding? Or would that bring up sad memories?" She tied on the new apron she'd recently purchased for the shop. Aunt

Doris refused to use one, preferring her much-used, ratty, multi-stained smock from when Christie's grandma Maude owned the shop. She claimed the new ones with the embroidered logo were too pretty to use for work.

"They're going to be sad no matter what, Christie. Just make them something beautiful and be sure to use some yellow and pink flowers. They're always happier than the darker colors. There are some beautiful mauve calla lilies in the cooler and yellow chrysanthemums. And I would add those dark blue delphiniums."

"Thanks, Auntie. Great ideas."

"You haven't answered my question about helping McAvoy."

"Well, he reluctantly gave me permission to interview the mother of the victim when he realized she might relate better to a female. He didn't get much information when he talked with her. So Anita and I drove up to Elida yesterday and met with her. Turns out she was actually the grandmother of the victim. Lauren was her name."

"Elida? What was a girl from Elida doing here in White Castle?"

"Well, more interesting than that is that Lauren had told her grandma that she was going to a wedding at the Lutheran church. So why was she at the mansion?"

"That's an equally good question."

"We talked to her friend Jazmine also. She told me some stuff about a boyfriend. I got the impression that Lauren wasn't very outgoing. She was still living at home and was already twenty-three years old."

"That's not unusual these days, as you very well know. Especially if she didn't have a job. Was she going to college?"

Christie shared that Lauren had recently finished an associate's degree and had started a new job. "She reminds me of one of the girls who lived in my dorm. Liz. She wasn't very outgoing and didn't participate in any of the activities that the rest of us enjoyed. I worried that she was depressed, not just a loner. Even the residential advisor tried to get her to consider counseling. She dropped out of school instead." Christie sighed. "I've always wondered if I could've reached her and helped if I'd persisted. Maybe Lauren had depression that was never treated."

The door chimed with the entry of a customer. Christie looked up to see that it was McAvoy instead. She quickly wiped her hands on the towel lying on the counter and whipped off her apron.

"Good morning, Detective. How can I help you? Do you need flowers or something for your receptionist?"

"Not a bad idea, but not today. She's out this week for a family wedding in California. And, of course, you know that the chief is out for that conference. I hope it's not going to be a crazy week." He removed his hat and placed it on the counter in front of him. "I came for the laptop."

"Oh, of course. It's right here." Christie reached into a drawer and pulled out the laptop, still in its protective plastic sleeve.

McAvoy tucked it under his arm. "I was doing some more thinking about what you told me. You said there had been another death at Langley Manor twenty-five years ago. And it had something to do with the caretaker who works there now."

"Yes, he told Anita and me that the girl who died was his niece. He lives there, hoping that her murderer will show up again someday."

McAvoy scoffed. "Really? Why would he think that? Especially after so much time has gone by."

"He said he promised his sister, the victim's mother, that he would never stop looking."

"I still seriously doubt there's any connection between the two cases, but it wouldn't hurt to look into that a little more. There's still the possibility Lauren's death wasn't an accident. I won't know for sure until I get the autopsy report. I'll talk with Jason, see if he wouldn't mind reviewing the old case files. Maybe he'll find something useful."

Christie beamed a smile at McAvoy, pleased that he was acting on her suggestion. And she wasn't about to mention that she'd already talked to Jason about just that. Now it would be official for them to research a bit more. "I'm sure he'd be happy to help."

"Great. Maybe I'll get flowers for Joyce next week when she's back. To tell her how much I appreciate having her at the front desk. At least I knew how to run the copy machine." He donned his hat and turned to leave.

"What about Drew and Tiffany?" Christie asked before he took a second step. "Were they helpful?"

McAvoy glanced back at the flower room before replying. "Max and I interviewed them separately, but neither of them gave us any useful information. They both denied knowing the young lady."

"There are some pictures on the laptop you're taking that I think will prove that at least one of them is lying. We saw a photo of Lauren with a guy that could be Adam, and another of Drew."

"You're sure it was Drew?"

Christie nodded. "Absolutely." She watched the detective hurry out of the store, presumably eager to open the device and see the pictures for himself.

She was grinning when she rejoined her aunt in the flower room.

"What's with the grin, young lady?"

"I can't help it. Yesterday, McAvoy wasn't interested in an old case and today he is. The first death is why the widow's walk access was padlocked in the first place. I think the caretaker, Slim Ferguson, put it there because of his niece. And Jason told me last night that he'd have his private investigator, Ben, look into it, and now it's official that he can do it with permission."

"That's good. I worry when you and Anita and even Jason get involved with these cases."

Christie smiled at her aunt. "I don't mean to cause you any worry. But I'd like to help in some way so Mrs. Elliott knows that someone besides the police cares enough to get to the bottom of why her granddaughter died."

# CHAPTER THIRTEEN

Christie was grateful for the busy morning with orders for table-top arrangements for a Chamber of Commerce luncheon in addition to the usual anniversary and birthday bouquets. There had been a death at the local nursing home, so she was pretty sure there would also be a spate of funeral flowers in the mix by the afternoon. In a few days, there could possibly be more for Lauren's funeral as well, depending on how the Elliotts handled their granddaughter's demise.

Her monthly receipts had continued to grow during the year and a half she'd been in business, despite the occasional hiccup. Her sideline landscaping business, Prestige Garden Design, which she shared with Anita, was also doing well despite the rough start when a boundary dispute erupted at their very first project.

When she'd first reopened her grandmother's florist business, she couldn't have predicted that it would flourish. She truly loved what she was doing compared to the ten years she'd spent working as an accountant for a big furniture business in San Francisco. Every now and then, she had to pinch herself and smile. She had a comfortable relationship with Jason Princeton, a high school classmate and now the town's primary attorney. Her parents didn't pressure her with questions about her future, although she knew they wanted to know if she and Jason would ever be "serious." They would just have to wait along with Christie. She wasn't sure herself if she wanted to be Mrs. Princeton. She was perfectly happy being Christie O'Mara, shopkeeper.

She snapped out of her reverie when the doorbell chimed. She looked up to see Jason, speaking, or more specifically, thinking of the devil, waltz in. She gave him a little wave and quickly finished the order she'd been working on.

"Hey," she said as she joined him at the order desk after she took off her work apron. "Did you hear from McAvoy today?"

"No. Why?"

"Good, because that means I get to tell you the news."

"What news?" He narrowed his eyes. "I hope it's the good kind. Did he get the autopsy report already? Has he decided that it was a murder after all?"

Christie shook her head and laughed. "I said it was news, not a miracle. It's about Lauren's death, as you guessed. He told me he was going to ask you to stop by his office and pick up the notes from an old case where another young girl died at the mansion. In a similar way, as it turns out." She gave him a sly look, since they'd already planned on this.

"I thought you said he wasn't interested in checking it out, so now I'm confused."

"He came by here a little earlier and said he'd thought more about it and decided to look into it after all. Well, actually, he wants *you* to look into it and tell him if there's anything worth pursuing. You will do it, won't you?"

"Sure. Like I mentioned, Ben gets a kick out of these old

cases and loves being able to get them solved. He's really an old soul."

"So why are you here, since it isn't about McAvoy's request for help?"

"I figured I'd take an early lunch so I could stop by and tell you what I'd found out about Drew and Tiffany so far. Pretty interesting."

"As in, how are they interesting?"

"Turns out that the groom, Drew, was previously engaged but broke it off after his father threatened to cut him out of his inheritance."

"That's kind of interesting, but I hope you have more than that."

"I do, as a matter of fact. That was only six months ago and here he is, marrying Tiffany already. She comes from a family that's connected to Big Oil and stands to inherit a lot of money someday."

"Are you suggesting that Drew married Tiffany for the money? Wouldn't she have suspected that?"

"You'd think so, but money still talks, at least in some circles. And you have to understand that the groom is also connected to money. His dad is an investor who hit it big when he made some shrewd purchases in the earlier tech days. He's big into cryptocurrency as well and apparently got lucky with that."

"What about financial issues that someone mentioned at the reception? Was that Drew?"

"Maybe. He managed to land a job with a financial company owned by one of his father's friends. He's managing a few accounts for them and obviously hopes to go up the ladder like his father did. But word is that he's spending a lot more money than he's making."

"And what does that have to do with Lauren?"

"That's who he was supposedly engaged to, according to what Ben discovered."

"You're kidding," said Christie. "Are you suggesting that the jilted ex-fiancée attends the wedding and gets herself murdered in the process? That doesn't sound like a good idea on her part. In the first place, she doesn't seem to be the kind of girl who would run in the same social circle as Drew Simpson likely does. Mrs. Elliott said she was shy and had few friends. Even the Elliotts' home indicates they don't swim in the same circle as Drew's family. Mrs. Elliott certainly never implied her granddaughter was engaged. And why would Lauren have an invitation to the wedding?"

"Maybe it wasn't meant for her," said Jason. "It could've been a mutual friend who offered it to her."

"Or did her creepy boyfriend somehow get one?"

"Good question. We may never know, unless we can find this Adam guy."

"I think Jazmine will come through with that," said Christie. "She said she knew how to reach him. She's going to tell him I'm interested in his ghost research."

"If he's at all narcissistic, that line could work."

"With that new information, I'm positive McAvoy will want to interview Drew again when he gets back from his honeymoon. And probably his parents as well."

"Hey, Christie. I need to get back to work. I have a new client coming in. I'll call you later."

"Okay. I need to help Aunt Doris create more floral baskets myself."

Aunt Doris peered over her half-glasses when Christie rejoined her in the flower room and put her work apron on again. "You said you weren't going to get involved, but if Jason is helping McAvoy, I'll bet you won't be able to help yourself, missy."

"It's not likely that I'm going to be in any danger, Auntie. I don't plan on going to any haunted houses in the near future." Christie winked at her aunt while pulling an order off the top of the stack. "This is another one for the Simpsons. I wonder why people are sending thank you bouquets just for being invited to a fancy wedding?" She sighed. "I hope Mrs. Elliott is getting flowers too. I think she deserves them more than these rich people. They didn't lose a precious granddaughter."

"It would be a nice gesture to take some flowers to her, just because," said her aunt.

Christie brightened. "That's a lovely idea, Auntie. I'll deliver them myself while Heather takes care of these other deliveries." She opened the door of the flower cooler and selected baby pink roses, white lilies, blue delphinium, and silvery eucalyptus.

Her aunt nodded appreciatively when she laid them on the table. "Your grandmother would be so proud of you for your kind heart and generosity." She wiped a tear from her eye. "I still miss her, you know."

Christie walked around the table to give her aunt a gentle hug. "So do I."

"What kind of written message are you planning to include? You can't get too personal with this one."

"How about this? 'May the fragrance of love and memory gently surround you, and may you always feel Lauren's presence in your heart.' "

"Perfect. Now, let's get going on these orders. I don't want to be working here till midnight."

# CHAPTER FOURTEEN

Christie called Anita, who was happy to ride shotgun for the visit to Mrs. Elliott.

"That's a gorgeous bouquet, Christie," Anita exclaimed when she saw it sitting on the dining table at Christie's home. "Mrs. Elliott is going to love it, especially when it's so unexpected." She snuggled Stormy, who had jumped onto the table to get some attention and scratches behind the ears.

"What's new with Joe?" Christie asked while signing a sympathy card to go with the flowers. "It's still weird to think about McAvoy as 'Joe.' "

Anita giggled. "I guess I didn't tell you the latest. We haven't had a chance to talk since yesterday, and that was all about Lauren."

Christie picked up the vase of flowers and walked to the door. "You can tell me about it on the way to Elida."

"Well, Joe wants me to meet his family. But I'm not sure about it. I mean, we've only been dating for a few months, and he's fun to be with and all, but I don't know that I'm ready to go that far. His parents live on Vashon Island, so it involves a ferry ride and schedules and all that."

"With them living that far away, it could involve an overnight stay too. Do you have cold feet or something?" Christie asked.

"I guess. I've been single for so long, I don't quite know what to think about a long-term relationship."

"Like Jason and me, you mean?"

"Yeah, like that. But at least you've known Jason since high school. We *all* knew each other. I don't know Joe well enough yet to think that far ahead."

"I get it. My parents drop hints now and then about my future, and I just give them a look. Jason doesn't pressure me at all. I think he likes it the way it is, at least for the foreseeable future."

Anita sighed. "You two seem very comfortable just being great friends."

Christie's phone rang. Jazmine's name popped up on the screen in her car. She punched the green phone icon. "Hi. This is Christie."

"Hey, this is Jazmine. Lauren's friend. Do you have a minute?"

"Sure. How can I help you?"

"I got Adam's contact information for you like you asked. I had to call other friends of his and finally convinced one of them that I wasn't going to turn him in or anything."

"Why did he think you would turn him in? For what?" Christie wrinkled her brow.

"Ethan said something about a break-in that Adam might have been involved in, but I didn't know anything about it. I told him I was trying to help Lauren's mom, I mean her grandma, with a funeral plan and that she wanted to be able to invite him."

Christie asked, "Is that true about the funeral plans?"

"Yes and no. She is planning a funeral, but she doesn't want to have anything to do with Adam, so I lied there. I had my fingers crossed behind my back when I said it." Jazmine giggled into the phone. "Anyway, I'll text you what I got from his friend. I don't know where he's living or anything like that. Ethan said there was some new stuff on his blog about ghosts, if you want to check it out. I'll send the link with his contact information."

"That would be wonderful, Jazmine. Thanks so much. I'm on my way right now to see Mrs. Elliott and deliver some flowers. She'll be happy to know I might be able to get in touch with Adam, especially if I can get him to talk."

"Good luck, Christie. I hope you find out who pushed Lauren down those stairs—if it turns out that's what happened, that is. I don't want to think it was Adam, but if it was, he deserves whatever he gets."

When the call ended, Christie handed the phone to Anita. "As soon as Jazmine sends the link, go ahead and open it."

It was another two or three minutes before they heard the *ping* of an incoming message. Anita hummed to herself while she navigated to Adam's channel and read the transcript. "You're not going to believe this, Christie. "

"What did you find?"

"Adam rambles on quite a bit at first about how ghosts are all around us and that we don't notice their presence because we're not paying attention. And that they're always trying to make themselves known to us."

"Why would they want to do that, for Pete's sake?" said Christie.

"He says that ghosts are trying to tell us that things aren't as they appear. That we shouldn't assume someone is guilty of a crime, for example, based on superficial evidence."

"Well, duh. Of course we shouldn't. It makes me wonder if he's trying to say that *he's* the person who's not guilty of a crime. Does he say anything more profound than that?"

"No, but he posted a picture of Langley Manor and claims it's one of the places where he's encountered ghosts."

Christie scoffed. "What's his proof? Maybe he's going to claim that the orange cat there is a ghost."

"Maybe, but he also claims he met a real ghost there the week before Lauren died."

"Hmm. It makes me wonder if he planned something that involved Lauren and this 'ghost' and that her death really was accidental. I don't want to think he intended for her to be hurt."

"You mean like something went wrong?"

"Exactly," Christie agreed. "What if he had an accomplice who was supposed to play the part of the ghost so he could blog about it and Lauren's death complicated his plan?"

"That sounds like a possibility. Shouldn't you talk to McAvoy about it?"

"Yes, but I'll wait till we talk to Mrs. Elliott. We're almost to Elida. I hope she remembers something more about Adam or if Lauren said anything else that sheds light on this whole situation."

"That would be nice."

"And I'll call Adam after we talk with Lauren's grandmother. I want to hear more from him about this ghost."

## CHAPTER FIFTEEN

A late model white Camry was parked at the Elliott home when Christie and Anita pulled up in front.

"Looks like she may have company," said Christie.

"It might be family, seeing as they're parked in the driveway. I think most casual visitors would park in the street," observed Anita.

"Let's find out." Christie gathered the bouquet and card and led the way up the sidewalk to the door. Just as she was about to press the doorbell, she heard a male voice say, "People are going to find out sooner or later, Theresa. This might be a good time to clear the air."

"No, James. Not yet. Shh. I think I hear someone at the door."

Christie pressed the doorbell and stepped back.

Mrs. Elliott answered after a single buzz. Her stoic face turned into a soft smile when she saw the stunning bouquet in Christie's arms. "Please come in, young ladies. Pastor Smith is here to talk about Lauren's service at the Baptist church across town. Perhaps you can help him a bit." She glanced at him with a worried look on her face.

Christie and Anita looked at each other with little shrugs. "We'll try," said Christie.

Pastor Smith stood next to the fireplace when the pair entered the living room and extended his hand. "I'm James Smith, pastor at Calvary Baptist across town."

Niceties dispensed with, as the girls took a seat, Christie asked, "What would you like to know, Pastor? We didn't know Lauren at all in person."

"Mrs. Elliott Lauren's mother, has given me what I need to know for her service. I'm curious about her manner of death because a question was raised about this having happened in a haunted mansion."

Christie swallowed the scoff that came to her throat. "We think that the only ghostly aspect is an orange cat that seems to have the run of the place. The kitty belongs to the caretaker, who told us it's a good mouser. It seemed to show up every time we heard any unusual sounds. But that's hardly anything that would imply a haunting."

"I see," said Pastor Smith. "Then there's no reason to think that Lauren was pushed down the stairs by a ghost, I suppose."

Christie shook her head. That was an angle she hadn't even considered. "I hardly think so. The detective is still investigating, but he thinks there was another person on the widow's walk with her. He just doesn't know who it was yet."

"How is he going to prove that there was someone up there with her?"

Anita said, "Ghosts don't leave footprints, sir."

Christie thought the pastor's face paled a bit as he said, "Of course not. I only bring it up because I've seen a handful of posts about ghosts at that building. And speculation about whether or not Lauren had been spooked, causing her to fall."

Christie said, "I'm sure Detective McAvoy would like to see those posts, if you don't mind sharing them. You can forward them to me, and I'll pass them on."

"I'll do that. I'd like to help in any way I can."

Christie found a business card in her wallet that she handed to the pastor. "My email address is right there, or you can use text if you prefer."

Pastor Smith examined the card. "Thank you. You're a florist, huh? Mrs. Elliott told me before you came that you were working with the police department on this. How does a flower shop owner get involved in police business?"

Christie laughed. "It's *because* of my flowers. They've been present at some of events where someone died or almost died. I've had to defend them when the police jumped to conclusions about my flowers being guilty in some way when I knew they were innocent."

Pastor Smith chuckled. "You talk about them as though they were people."

Christie felt her body tense. "It's really my business reputation that I'm defending. The flowers are simply my face to the world. I hope to stay in business a long time, so it's important that the police determine what really happened. Because I was the floral decorator, I suspect some blame will be tossed my way. It's happened before."

"Well, I certainly didn't have any idea about any of that." Pastor Smith's tanned face seemed to redden. "I'm sorry to have touched a sensitive topic."

"It's really okay, Pastor. Lauren's situation reminds me of a girl in my dorm who seemed to have very few friends. I can't bring Mrs. Elliott's daughter back, but at least I can help find out what really happened. She deserves that."

"Yes... Uh, of course," he stammered.

"I'll forward those posts to Detective McAvoy as soon I get them from you."

The pastor made no motion to leave, no doubt with more funeral arrangements to discuss, so the girls stood to leave.

Mrs. Elliott walked to the door with them. "Thank you for coming by. I have a feeling you'll get to the bottom of this. I don't want people to have the wrong idea about my Lauren. I'm sure she was innocent of any wrongdoing." She wiped a tear from her eye with an old-fashioned handkerchief that she pulled out of the sleeve of her long-sleeved blouse. "I would like it if you kept me informed."

"Yes, Mrs. Elliott," said Christie. "I do have another question. Is it possible that Lauren was engaged to someone—say, Drew Simpson—about six months ago?"

Mrs. Elliott furrowed her brow. "That name sounds familiar, but she's—was—very close-mouthed about her personal life." She was silent for a moment. "There was a period of time when she seemed to go out more often than usual and seemed happier than she used to be. That was late last summer, but I thought she was just going out with some of her classmates from the college."

"Could she have been seeing a guy instead?"

"I really don't know, but maybe. She'd never had a steady boyfriend before, not even in high school." She shook her head. "Now I realize I could have asked more questions, but she'd never been one to confide in me very much. I've always felt she wanted her real mom in her life instead of me." She sighed with her lips tight.

"I'm sure you did what you thought was best for her, Mrs. Elliott." Christie reached out and touched her arm. "Thank you for telling me a little more about Lauren. I feel a responsibility to your daughter to find out what really happened at Langley Manor."

Once they were on the road again, Christie said, "Something felt off with that pastor. Granted, I've never been much of a churchgoer, at least not since Mom made me go to Sunday school when I was a kid. But his demeanor gave me the willies." She glanced at Anita. "Did you sense anything weird?"

Anita shrugged. "Not really. He seemed overly friendly, but that might be normal for preachers and reverend-types. Always looking for more parishioners, I guess."

"Just before I hit the doorbell, I heard him say something about, 'People are going to find out something sooner or later,' and she said, 'Not yet, James.' He called her Theresa. What doesn't she want people to find out?"

"That *is* strange. I mean, they'll all know she died falling down stairs at Langley Manor—that certainly will be public knowledge. I have no idea, but it might not even be related to Lauren."

"And why would he be interested in ghosts? That seems strange for a religious person."

Anita laughed. "It's just that suspicious mind of yours, Christie. He's consoling her over the loss of her granddaughter. Maybe you're reading too much into it."

"Maybe. Probably. But he said something about Lauren maybe being pushed down those stairs. Most people are still assuming it was an accident, I think. Was he there? Were those his footprints?" Christie's phone pinged. She tossed it to Anita and said, "Will you check and see if that's a message from the pastor?"

"Yes. It looks like a link to something on X. Shall I open it?"

"Go ahead. I don't have an account on that media, but maybe it'll open anyway."

"Got it." Anita was quiet for a moment while she scrolled

through the messages. “This is definitely strange stuff about seeing ghosts around the area.” She continued to read through the posts. “This one says Adam can prove there was a ghost at Langley Manor and is inviting people to meet him there when he exposes the ghost.”

“What? Is he nuts?”

“Could be,” replied Anita, “but not crazy enough to put a date or time on this post.”

“Then how would his followers know when and where this is going to happen?” Christie sighed. “McAvoy can have the post traced, I hope, and track down Adam. Maybe he’ll be able to shed some light on what happened on Saturday. Ghosts, indeed.”

# CHAPTER SIXTEEN

Tuesday was a relatively quiet day at the flower shop. A few more orders were called in for the funeral later in the week. Christie checked the weekend calendar and noticed that White Castle High School's prom was scheduled for Saturday night. In addition to her typical order, she added flowers for the boutonnières and corsages that would be requested for the occasion. She'd learned during her first year in business to keep more in stock than she thought she would need. There were always a few last-minute pleas from desperate teenage boys who had forgotten to order ahead, and she hated to disappoint the young girl of their dreams.

After she finished the warehouse order, Christie picked up the notebook she'd been using to jot down her thoughts about Lauren's death, whether or not it was a murder, and the mansion in general. She puzzled over the two sets of footprints they'd found on the widow's walk. Both she and McAvoy had assumed they belonged to Lauren and the boyfriend, but what if that was an incorrect conclusion? She felt pretty certain that the smaller print belonged to a girl, and Lauren seemed like the perfect fit.

But the larger print, in fact both of them, could have been made at different times, though still very recently. And there was nothing that could specifically identify them as belonging to any particular person. Unless there had been an identifiable tread—such as on a Nike or Converse sport shoe—that could at least narrow down the possibilities. Christie picked up her phone to call McAvoy.

"McAvoy here. How can I help you, Christie?"

Christie was mildly surprised that the detective had her contact information in his phone considering that he probably had a whole raft of contacts. "Hey, Detective McAvoy. I had some new suspect ideas. I just had a thought about the shoe prints we found at the mansion. Did you notice a tread that could identify the brand of shoe? I was thinking of ways to narrow down the field of men that the larger prints could belong to."

"That's a good thought. Let me scroll through the photos and look more carefully. I don't recall anything jumping out at me when I first saw them, however."

It was a long moment before McAvoy spoke again. "I'll run these footprints through the identification system, but they look too smudged to be useful. I suppose there's an off chance there could be something here that's specific to a brand name, but right now I'd have to say that these could be almost any shoe with a pattern on the sole."

Christie sighed. "I was hoping they'd be more helpful than that. Can I ask if you've been able to talk to the boyfriend, Adam something?"

"Not yet. The first number was out of service, but I do have another phone number and names of places to check where he's been known to hang out."

"Well, good luck, McAvoy."

"You mentioned other suspect ideas. Do you have anyone in particular in mind?"

"No, but I'm wondering why Pastor Smith has such an interest in Adam's blogposts. I met him at Mrs. Elliott's when they were planning Lauren's funeral."

"I haven't met Pastor Smith yet. What can you tell me about him?"

Christie shared her thoughts that the minister seemed a little cozier with Lauren's grandmother than normal for a funeral planning visitation. "Something tells me he knows Adam personally or has some connection to him—more than just following the blog."

"Sounds like I better follow up on him. With Chief Conway out this week, I'll have Officer Newell visit him. He's in Elida, you said?"

"Yes. I believe he's at the Baptist church there. It's such a tiny town, I doubt there's more than one of them. He should be easy to track down."

McAvoy agreed. "I should have Newell call the church before he heads up that way. In case he needs to schedule an appointment. Thanks, Christie."

As she pocketed her phone, Christie thought again for a moment about the minister and the ghost blog posts. She couldn't come up with a logical explanation for his interest. She was familiar with the Trinity and the Holy Ghost, but that didn't seem relevant.

"What did the detective say, Christie?" Aunt Doris asked from the flower room. "Did he give you another assignment? He should be doing the detecting, not asking you to help." She harrumphed loudly to make her point.

Christie joined her aunt and put on her work apron. "He's going to follow up on Pastor Smith and the footprints we found at the mansion. I don't have to do anything, Auntie. And he's not saying anything about my murderous flowers this time," she said with a tiny shrug and a smile.

"But you're going to do something, aren't you?" Doris peered over her half-moon glasses. "I know you can't leave it alone when you feel responsible, even if it's a ridiculous thought."

"Well, I was kinda thinking about that fence that Mom mentioned between the old high school that was torn down and the mansion. She said that the high school boys used to sneak through the fence and smoke to avoid getting caught doing it on the school grounds."

"I don't understand what that would prove, honey."

"Slim—I mean, Mr. Flanagan, the caretaker—mentioned that he has to chase ghost hunters off the property now and then. There has to be another way for them to get on the grounds when the main gate is locked. Maybe it's through the old fence."

"Okay, but what does that have to do with the incident on Saturday?"

"I'm not sure yet, but I want to check the fence myself. I'm sure McAvoy would laugh if I mentioned it to him without having checked myself whether or not it was a possible point of access without going through the main entrance either to get in or to escape. He's extra busy anyway, with Chief Conway and his receptionist, Joyce, both gone this week. I'm sure Anita will go with me if I ask."

Christie knew her aunt was rolling her eyes without even looking at her.

~

Anita was, of course, game to search the fence. She met Christie after they were both done with work for the day.

"What's your plan for checking that fence if we find the gate to the driveway locked?" she asked as they drove up the winding road toward the entrance.

"We're not going to go in that way," said Christie. "Mom told Jason and me at dinner on Sunday that she'd heard about the high school boys going through holes in the school's fence to smoke when she was kid. That building was torn down back in the nineties. When the developer built all those condos on the hill, he probably didn't bother to check beyond those trees. The trees and underbrush are already a natural barrier. I doubt he was even concerned about whether or not there was a fence in the trees on the property line."

"Are you thinking that we can get through the fence from behind the condos?" Anita asked. "Isn't that going to be private property?"

Christie shrugged. "Maybe, but I'm not planning to enter from the condominiums' parking lots. I figured we would start our search from where the gate spans the main driveway and follow the fence line around. I know that the trees totally hide the mansion from view from the highway now and that the building was visible from there many years ago. The trees are probably growing on both sides of the fence and will hide us from being seen from the condos, as well as from the mansion."

"This sounds pretty sneaky to me, Christie. Now I know why you told me to wear my old shoes!"

"Here we are." Christie parked the car in a wide space along the road about 100 yards from the gate of Langley Manor's driveway. She retrieved a small bag from the trunk and slung it over her shoulder. Slamming the lid shut, she said, "Let's go exploring."

"What's in the bag?"

"A few tools we might need, plus a flashlight."

"Tools? Why would we need tools?"

"I brought pliers, a wire-cutter, and a short-handled lopper just in case we encounter too much underbrush to move."

"Why would we need pliers and a wire-cutter for that? There's supposed to be some kind of way to get through already." She gave Christie a suspicious look.

"Well, I wanted to be prepared, just in case. I suppose we could still use them as weapons if we run into unfriendly interlopers."

Anita groaned and followed Christie up the road to the closed gate. Unseen, they slipped into the shadowy space between the trees to the right and the fence on their left.

# CHAPTER SEVENTEEN

It was light enough that Christie and Anita were able to see a faint path for the first several hundred feet or so. Soon, however, the trees were so dense that the early evening light wasn't strong enough to penetrate the firs and cedars that lined both sides of the fence. Even the deciduous oaks and elms were fully leafed out, adding to the shade cover.

"We might as well be in the middle of a big forest," said Anita. "I can't see a thing more than a few feet ahead. Good thing you brought that flashlight."

"It was a last minute thought. The flashlights on our cell phone cameras would help some, but they don't throw off as long a beam," said Christie.

"How far along this fence do you think we'll have to go before we're in line with the house itself?" Anita asked as she trudged behind her friend. "I don't have a good sense of how it's laid out."

"I looked at it using the satellite view of the map earlier today. I figured it would be an eight- to ten-minute walk at a normal pace."

"Which this isn't because of all the undergrowth and fallen trees in our way," said Anita. "At least the loppers have been useful to get some of the branches out of the way."

"True." Christie stopped to look at her GPS map. "We should be getting close. If I'm calculating correctly, we'll be directly between the old high school and the mansion right about..." She walked another hundred feet or so along the trail. "Here."

Christie stopped and looked through the underbrush toward the fence line some twenty feet away.

"It certainly looks like there's a trail through from here to the fence. It's partially overgrown by blackberry vines, but I think we can follow it," she said.

"You lead. I'll follow. After all, *you* were the Girl Scout. I flunked Brownies."

They shared a laugh before plunging through the trees with Christie in front using the flashlight and loppers. The trail was easy to pick out despite the dense overgrowth. Someone, or perhaps multiple someones, had been using it recently enough to keep the trail useable.

"Are we there yet?" Anita asked after a few minutes. "We should've brought bread crumbs, by the way, like Hansel and Gretel."

"Squirrels would eat them," said Christie.

After another few feet they reached the fence, then followed it for about thirty feet until they found an opening in the heavy-duty chain link material. At some point, someone had cut through the fence and pulled it open, wide enough for a person to climb through. The metal had rusted with time and the opening had been partially reclaimed by blackberry vines.

"Somebody has cut these recently," said Christie, pointing to several places where the vines were freshly severed.

"This certainly could be the access point for someone to get on the grounds without going through the gate," said Anita.

"Yes, like Lauren's murderer or co-conspirator."

Anita felt something scurry across her foot. "I'm getting the willies. Are you sure being here is a good idea?" she whispered, her voice barely above the sound of the wind coming up from the river.

"No, but I'm going to take a few pictures to show McAvoy that we know it can be done," Christie said quietly.

"Did you bring something we can use to mark it, just in case?"

"Not necessary," said Christie. "We know it's here, and I'll tell McAvoy where it is from the GPS marking. I want to go a little farther along the fence."

"Why? Isn't this far enough?"

"Maybe. But I still want to see if there's a place where a trail leads up from the condos below that connects to the fence."

They'd gone only a few feet farther when faintly—almost too soft to notice—came the sound of music. Not a radio, not the wind, but a slow, lilting waltz drifting from somewhere high above. The notes rose and fell like sighs caught in a fog.

Anita clutched Christie's arm. "Do you hear that?"

Christie nodded, her pulse quickening. "It came from the direction of the mansion," she whispered back.

A beat of silence followed—and then, somewhere in the darkened house beyond the trees, an invisible shutter slammed against a wall.

"I want to go back now," said Anita. "I don't care if there's a trail from the condo."

"You're right. We can stop here and go back," said Christie. "McAvoy can check out the rest of the fence line if he wants to, but we've proven that there is at least one other route onto the property."

Anita walked close to Christie, almost stepping on her heels, as they retraced their steps. "And this is important because...?"

"It opens the door for other suspects—those who weren't there for the wedding or catering, most specifically. We need to find out why Lauren was really there and *how* she got there, if we can. She had that invitation for a reason, I'm sure. Maybe she knew about that opening in the fence and snuck in by herself."

"What about the padlock? How did she get up to the widow's walk if it was locked?"

Christie shook her head. "I don't know yet, but I'm sure she had some kind of help."

"I wouldn't call it a very nice kind of help when she ended up dead," said Anita with a hint of anger in her usually calm voice.

"I doubt that was part of the plan."

"So what was the plan? And whose plan was it?"

"Adam comes to mind. Somehow, I think it's connected to his ghost blogs and the other big plans that Jazmine mentioned." Christie stopped in her tracks. "Ethan. Adam's friend that Jazmine contacted. Ethan might know something that could help us figure it out, even if he doesn't realize that he does."

"Uh, Christie. You're not making sense again. How could he know something but not know that he knows it?"

"What I mean is that Ethan may have some other tidbit of information that makes sense when you connect it to other bits of evidence. But not by itself."

"Do you think he'll talk to you?"

"Why wouldn't he? He seemed to care about Adam as a

friend. Adam hasn't been officially identified as a suspect at this point, even if he's a person of interest. McAvoy isn't going to release any information to the public until he gets the autopsy report, so for now, this is still an unfortunate accidental death."

"But not in your eyes."

"Correct. Or at least, not a straightforward, simple accidental death. It appears that something happened that wasn't supposed to. We just need to figure out what that was." Christie turned to smile triumphantly at Anita as they exited the trees at the point where they'd entered thirty minutes earlier.

Christie stopped and held her arm out. "Wait a second, Anita. I can hear the manor's gate opening."

They slunk back into the shadow of the trees and waited. A silver SUV drove through the gate, a mere fifty feet in front of them, and continued down the street. They waited a minute while the gate screeched closed, and still another minute before hustling to Christie's car down the road.

Christie's heart thumped in her chest and her hands trembled while she started the engine.

"That was Pastor Smith," she said. "What was he doing up here?"

"And he's driving a silver SUV," added Anita. "I think it was a Subaru."

# CHAPTER EIGHTEEN

Christie handed her phone to Anita and asked her to call McAvoy.

"What will I tell him?"

"Exactly what happened. The most important part is that we saw Pastor Smith leaving the mansion in a silver SUV. I want McAvoy to find out why he was there."

"Wasn't he in a Camry when we met him at the Elliotts' home?" Anita asked as she located McAvoy's name in the contact list.

"Yes. One of the cars could belong to someone else. McAvoy can find out."

McAvoy answered after two rings. "Hey, Christie. What's going on?"

"It's Anita, Joe. I'm on Christie's phone because she's driving."

"Okay. What kind of trouble did she get you into this time?"

"We're not in trouble—at least not yet." Anita giggled nervously. She glanced sideways at Christie. "We were checking the fence at Langley Manor to see if there was a way to get onto the property without going up the driveway and we just saw Pastor Smith, you know, the minister from Elida, driving away. Christie asked me to tell you."

"Driving away from where?"

"From the mansion. He came through the gate and drove back down the hill toward town."

"Why is that important? I'm not understanding what it has to do with anything, Anita."

Anita turned to Christie and rolled her eyes, pointing to the phone. "When Christie and I met with Mrs. Elliott, Lauren's grandmother, the second time, this guy, Pastor Smith, was there. We both had a weird feeling about him, and now it looks like he's connected somehow to whatever is going on up there."

"Do you mean that you and Christie think something is going on at the mansion that involves the pastor?"

"Yes. Maybe."

Anita heard a long sigh on the other end of the phone and pictured McAvoy rubbing his head.

"Christie—I mean, we—think you should talk to him and find out why he was there. It could be perfectly innocent, but it seems suspicious. Especially to Christie." She turned to see Christie glaring at her. "And he was driving a silver SUV this time. He had a white Camry when we saw him yesterday."

"Okay. Tell Christie I'll have Newell look into it. I'll call you later tonight."

"Will do. And thanks." Anita handed the phone back.

"What did he say? Is he going to investigate Pastor Smith?"

"Um, he said to tell you he'd have Officer Newell talk to him."

"That's all?

"Yeah. That's all there was about Pastor Smith."

"But he said something else," said Christie. "I can read your face, you know."

Anita's face immediately reddened. "He said he'd call me later tonight. That's it."

"Oh. Do you have time to have a glass of wine at my house before you go home? Your car's there already."

"Yes, I'd like that."

"Me too."

STORMY WAS WAITING at the door when Christie and Anita returned from their excursion. The domestic shorthair ran into the kitchen and jumped onto the counter next to the kitty food jar and sat down like the Queen of Sheba. She waited impatiently for her mistress to fill her bowl with a handful of kibble plus some of her favorite canned salmon, then hopped down to the floor to eat when Christie was finally done.

"She really gobbles that food down," said Anita.

"Yeah. You'd think she's worried she'll never get another meal," said Christie. "Why don't you open this bottle of cabernet while I get the glasses out?"

Settled in the living room on the sofa, with flames dancing in the natural gas fireplace, the friends toasted each other.

"Here's to finding another piece of this puzzle," said Christie.

"Even if we don't know how it fits," said Anita.

"Speaking of pieces not fitting," said Christie after several swallows of wine, "I'm having trouble figuring out why Lauren was there in the first place, let alone why she ended up dead. I can't believe that anyone intended for her to die, but I could be wrong."

"In that sense, maybe hers was a truly accidental death, but someone is still guilty of something."

"I agree, but was it murder?"

Stormy joined them on the sofa with a soft meow that sounded like a rolled "r." The kitty rarely actually meowed like normal cats, Christie had noticed, unless she was seriously upset.

Christie stroked her silky, soft fur while Stormy purred on her lap. "Let's think of reasons that Lauren may have been at the wedding," she said.

"She had an invitation, for one thing," began Anita, "although we don't know if it was really hers, or how she got it if it wasn't meant for her."

"Mrs. Elliott mentioned that she'd talked about going to a wedding with Adam, but it didn't sound like it was the right one. And it sounded like she didn't want to go. Why would that be?"

"There was that text or email about some kind of lock," said Anita.

"Yes, but that could've referred to the widow's walk lock or the main gate, which doesn't really make sense... or some other lock we don't know about."

It was quiet for a moment as the fire danced and the girls sipped their wine.

"I wonder if it's true that Drew, the bridegroom, had been engaged to Lauren," Christie mused. "He certainly seems out of her league, but it wouldn't be impossible. And she might have wanted to see the lucky girl he was marrying."

"Do you think Drew might have sent her the invitation?"

Christie shook her head. "No, it seems to me more like something a vengeful woman might do. Tiffany would be my guess, if it was an official invitation. But Lauren might still have gotten it from a mutual friend. We need to find out who

Tiffany's and Drew's other friends are and find out more about what they're like."

"Didn't you say you'd met Tiffany's maid of honor, Stephanie? She might be willing to talk with us—I mean, you." Anita poured herself another bit of wine from the bottle sitting on the coffee table.

"And there's still Adam, who seems to have disappeared into the woodwork. He could've gotten one and given it to Lauren the day of the wedding as a surprise that turned out to be a deadly mistake." Christie handed her glass to Anita. "I'll take some of that wine now. When you talk to McAvoy—I just can't call him Joe yet—will you ask him if he or Newell have been able to locate Adam? And if they've interviewed the groomsmen more thoroughly than the few minutes they spent doing it at the reception?"

"I suppose you want me to ask if you can talk with all these people as well."

"Not really. Since none of them are official suspects, I don't think I need permission to just talk to them," said Christie.

"I'm not going to tell Joe anything about you possibly doing unofficial interviews. He'll tell me to tell you to stay out of the detecting business. Again."

"Whatever happened to being considered innocent until proven guilty?" said Christie with an angelic look on her face.

# CHAPTER NINETEEN

Christie had barely unlocked her front door for business Wednesday morning when Detective McAvoy marched in. He looked like someone ready to fight. Stormy usually hopped down from her perch to get some kitty love when he came in, but she must have sensed his mood. She drew her ears back, sat on her haunches, and stayed on her shelf instead.

"You look like you're all business this morning, Detective," said Christie as she met him at the counter. "Is something wrong?" In the past, when she'd first come to town, if he bounded in like this it was something he perceived that she'd done wrong. Like interview with his cases. She held her breath.

McAvoy pulled an envelope from his jacket pocket and removed the small sheaf of papers. He handed them to Christie. "You can skip to the end of the third page, where the pathologist lists the presumed cause of death."

Christie quickly scanned the first two pages anyway—she didn't believe in shortcuts. Her eyes widened when she got to the section with the final impression. "Death by asphyxiation due to strangulation; secondary fracture of cervical spine causing brainstem injury, consistent with a fall down a flight of stairs." She looked up at McAvoy. "I presume you'll have to call it a murder after all, even if the fall itself was an accident."

McAvoy nodded grimly. "Officer Newell and I will be busy with more interviews. I'd hoped it would be a simple accidental death, although there's never really anything simple about that."

He seemed surprised at the autopsy's findings. Christie didn't recall noticing any bruises on Lauren's neck, but the young victim had been wearing a high-neck, Victorian-style dress, which would have hidden any marks. Having been declared "dead on arrival," it was unlikely that McAvoy ever saw her again before she was sent for the autopsy, so he wouldn't have had the opportunity to see them either.

McAvoy returned the papers to the envelope and stuffed it in his jacket. "With this turn of events, I need to talk to Newell about doing more interviews. By the way, Jason picked up the file I mentioned earlier and said he'd get back to me soon."

"That's good. What about the boyfriend, Adam? Have you found him yet?"

"No, but with this now being a murder, I'll have Newell double down on finding him."

"Good luck, McAvoy," said Christie as he stomped out, clearly still disturbed about the turn of events. She sighed. At least he wasn't upset with her, but she almost wished it had been that instead of such a gruesome turn of events for poor Lauren.

Stormy chose that moment to jump down to the counter and get kitty love from her mistress.

Christie felt sad at the realization that Lauren had died a more traumatic death than had appeared on the surface. She'd truly hoped it would turn out to be an accident caused by the fall down the stairs, whether or not she'd been pushed. Being strangled cast a darker mood on the incident. She gave Stormy one more hug and lifted the kitty back to her observation post. She stiffened her back and walked to the flower room, where her aunt was busily making tabletop arrangements for a luncheon at the Lutheran church.

"Aunt Doris, do you remember anything about a young woman dying at Langley Manor? It would've been in the late nineties, I think, back when the old high school was adjacent to that property."

"Yes, Christie. It was the talk of the town for several weeks. As I recall, there was some discussion about a cover-up of some kind. There were those who were sure that one of the sons of the family had been involved, but in the end it was declared an accidental death. The police weren't able to come up with enough evidence to charge anyone. Why are you bringing that up?"

"I talked to the caretaker, Slim Flanagan—his real name is Larry—who told me that it was his niece who had died there. He's convinced she was murdered and that it was someone from inside the family, or a close friend of one of the sons. He's been there working all these years in case the murderer ever comes back. He's sure he would recognize him."

Doris shook her head with its frizzy halo of red hair. "Langley Manor was sold shortly after that incident, if I remember correctly. There was too much scandal and hateful talk for the family to stay in town, so they up and left. If one of those boys was involved, I can't imagine why he would take the risk of returning to the scene, even—or maybe especially—after all these years."

"Detective McAvoy just showed me the autopsy papers of the girl who died last weekend. She'd been strangled before she was 'helped' down those stairs."

"Oh, Christie. That's sad. Now the detective has a real murder on his hands. But let's get busy with these flowers that need to go out when Heather comes in this afternoon to do deliveries. We have about thirty corsages and boutonnières to do as well, because they'll be picked up on Thursday and Friday. I thought we could get a head start on those today, once we get these funeral orders out of the way."

But Christie couldn't let the subject go quite yet. "Did you know the family who owned Langley Manor when the first girl died? Do you remember anything about them or their friends?"

"I'll have to think about it. It was twenty-five years ago, after all. Hand me those ribbons, the gold ones."

Christie wondered why her aunt was stalling. Doris had a memory like the proverbial elephant. She knew everyone and everything that had ever happened around White Castle. And she was usually more than happy to share.

# CHAPTER TWENTY

After giving it some thought, Christie decided to go back to search the widow's walk again for anything that might have been missed the first time, considering that the official cause of death was no longer a straightforward accidental fall.

First things first, she called the caretaker to arrange admission to the grounds and the building. "Hey, Slim. This is Christie O'Mara from the Flower Shoppe. I've been working with Detective McAvoy, and I'd like to look at the widow's walk again, if you don't mind letting me into the building. And if you think it would be okay with Mrs. Lindemann."

"Sure, missy. What time do you need me to open the gate?"

She timed her next call so it would be during Anita's lunch period. Anita agreed to join her in a bit of sleuthing that evening.

The gate to Langley Manor was open when Christie and Anita arrived shortly before 6:30. Slim met them at the bottom of the wide stairs that resembled the Georgian plantation home the manor had been modeled after.

"I feel like Scarlett O'Hara every time I see this gorgeous building," said Christie. "I wonder if the wife of the original owner felt the same way when she first saw it."

"If I remember the story correctly, they lost the home not that many years later in a sheriff's sale," said Anita. "That would've been a very sad day, I'm sure."

"What are you looking for this time, Miss O'Mara?" Slim asked, getting to the point of their visit.

"I'm not sure, but I'm hoping to find something—anything—that could explain why Lauren was here in the first place. And please call me Christie."

"Will do. I've unlocked the door for you. When you're done, drive around to my cottage and let me know so I can close up behind you."

"Of course."

Slim turned to walk to his cottage on the other side of the property. Christie noticed that he was walking without a limp.

"Hey Slim!" she called out before he was out of sight.

"Yeah? What is it?" he said when he turned around.

"You're not limping today like you did on Saturday."

Slim reached down to rub his knee. "This old knee acts up some days more than others. And I don't always remember to take the medicine the doctor prescribed." He stood up and hitched his jeans up. "Today's a good day now that it's getting a little warmer." He saluted, just touching the brim of his cowboy hat, and turned back to his home.

Christie shrugged and said to Anita, "That makes sense, I guess."

A moment later, Christie and Anita scrambled up the stairs, ten in all, to the double-door entrance. Slim had left the door open to the grand foyer. They crossed the ballroom to the stairs that led to the second level, then the third level. The padlock had been set aside, so they were able to open the hatch door at the top of the ladder-like stairs to the widow's walk. Christie climbed the steps first and lifted the door out of the way. It was already twilight, so she used her flashlight in the semi-dark. The footprints she'd seen earlier were now scuffed and unidentifiable. She guessed that had occurred during the investigation when several people could have been on the walkway.

"I'll search going one way and you can go the other way," said Christie. "I don't know what I expect to find, but I have to look." She reached into her pocket and handed a second flashlight to Anita.

The two young women walked slowly along the forty-foot walkway, peering under the ledge and brushing their hands below the rolled handrail.

"There isn't much of a place where anything could be hidden," Anita pronounced.

"I agree," said Christie. "I'm not finding anything at all. Let's go back down and search the next level more carefully. Maybe something else dropped out of her hands when she fell. She was likely unconscious, if not dead, before she hit the floor, and she wouldn't have been able to hold onto anything."

"Which is why we found the invitation on the floor instead of in her hands," added Anita, nodding.

"Exactly."

Christie pulled the trapdoor closed behind her and followed Anita back down. They walked opposite directions from the ladder to either end of the hall-like space, using their flashlights to augment the single ceiling light.

"I feel like a real detective," said Anita. "You know how they always depict them using flashlights in unlit rooms on television. I've often wondered why someone doesn't just turn on the lights!"

Christie laughed. "It wouldn't be the same effect. They're going for the drama of it all."

She went around a corner and jumped when she encountered the ginger tabby cat. It was stretched out, scratching at the floor. "Have you found a mouse there, Mr. Kitty Cat?" She knelt to pet the cat and out of the corner of her eye saw the edge of a piece of paper peeking out from underneath the baseboard a foot away.

She reached for it with one hand while stroking the cat's head with the other.

"I might have something here," she called. She carefully teased the small piece of paper out from its hiding place, then sat down on the floor, holding it by one corner to avoid any further fingerprint contamination. It was a photocopy of an old newspaper clipping.

Anita joined her as Christie read the headline. "It says, 'Victim of fall may have been pregnant.' "

"I assume it's referring to Slim's niece. Is there a date?"

"No, but the article names her as Debra Ellen Lewis, so it has to be a news article from twenty-five years back." She read further. "It says that an autopsy hadn't been done because it was clear it had been an accidental fall that caused her death. The reporter says the victim's mother was quite adamant that her daughter had told her she thought she might be pregnant."

"That puts a different spin on things," said Anita. "This may be part of what Lauren found in her search of the newspaper archives. But why would she have it with her here?"

Christie slipped the scrap of paper between two pages in the notebook she always carried in her jacket. She smiled at she realized she'd picked up the habit of always having one handy from Detective McAvoy. "It makes me wonder if Debra Ellen had told the father of the baby and stirred something up. And ended up dead because of it."

"I can kinda understand why the family left town. Even though today it isn't that big of a deal for that kind of thing, it probably was more shameful back at that time."

"The family that owned Langley Manor may have worried about its reputation, depending on who in the family was the purported culprit, if it was a family member at all," cautioned Christie. "Or if it was even true."

"Do you think Slim might know? Debra Ellen was his niece, after all."

"We can ask when we let him know we're done here."

The two young women made their way back to the main floor, the ginger tabby following behind them. They were careful to pull the door closed behind them. The tabby cat sat like a sentinel, its tail keeping time with an invisible clock.

## CHAPTER
# TWENTY-ONE

Christie and Anita crossed the freshly mown lawn to Slim's cottage beyond the parking lot. He sat in a wooden Adirondack chair that had once been bright red, can of beer in hand, one leg crossed over the other.

"Have a seat," he said, pointing to a bench next to his chair. "Did you find anything in your search?" He took a long swallow of his beer and wiped his mouth with the back of his hand. "They didn't find anything at all back when Debra Ellen was killed."

Christie opened the notebook to where she'd placed the clipping. Holding it in place with a finger over one corner, she held it so Slim could read it.

He leaned over, and his eyes widened when he recognized its significance. "Where did you find this?"

"It was on the third floor near where Lauren was found," said Christie. "It must have slipped from her hand when she fell and then got wedged under the baseboard behind the ladder."

Slim stood and set his beer on the arm of the chair. "I'll be right back."

He returned a few minutes later with a black three-ring binder. He sat down and flipped through the pages until he found what he wanted. He handed it to Christie. "Read this article and the one on the next page too."

Christie and Anita did as he asked. The first clipping was the same as they'd found in the building. The second one was a follow-up that had been written two weeks later, according to the dates that Slim had written above each article. The police had concluded that Debra Ellen's fall had been accidental and were still looking for a friend of the family as a "person of interest" for questioning.

"Do you know if the police at the time ever identified that person?" Christie closed the binder and handed it back.

"Not as far as I know. They pretty much decided by then that there wasn't enough evidence to point to any one individual. The family members had all been cleared. And by then, as you saw in the second article, the official cause of death was listed as 'an accidental fall' down those same stairs. They also suggested that Debra Ellen was possibly intoxicated, contributing to her injuries." He shook his head, his face grim. "I'm sure she wouldn't have been drinking at all if she thought she was pregnant."

Christie crossed one leg over the other, her elbows resting on a knee. "I know you've had a long time to think about this, Slim. What do *you* think really happened? Do you have a name?"

Slim took another draw from his beer. He wiped his mouth with the sleeve of his plaid shirt. "I think she probably told the father of the baby that she was worried she might be pregnant. That's what she told her mother, Dotty, and then Dotty told me, but not till afterward. I don't know which of the sons—there were three in all, but one of them was only fourteen at the time, so it probably wasn't him—would have been the guilty party. I never found out from Dotty which of the older boys she suspected before she died. And there was one friend of the oldest boy who hung around like he was family. I didn't live here in the cottage then, and the Donaldsons were gone by the time I arrived, so I never heard his name."

"How did you convince Mrs. Lindemann to let you live here in the cottage?" Christie asked gently. "I don't understand why she would agree to that, although you told me earlier you'd promised your sister to keep looking for your niece's murderer."

"Well, it was Dotty's idea, really. One of her friends was well acquainted with the lady of the house, Mrs. Donaldson. And when the Donaldsons decided to sell the place and move out of town, they sold it to Norma Lindemann. She had money from when her husband died and had wanted to have a place for weddings and the like. She didn't plan to be here full-time and when Mrs. Donaldson suggested that it would be wise to have a caretaker on the premises, Mrs. Lindemann agreed."

"Did the new owner know that it was your niece who had died here?"

"It never came up. If she knew, she never said anything about it and neither did I. Since she was from out of town, up Olympia way, she probably didn't have any idea about the situation. And she might not have cared."

"I see," said Christie as Anita nodded. "That makes total sense, I suppose."

"And I never asked for a lot of money. I'm a disabled veteran and had enough income to get by as long as I didn't have to pay too much for housing. She let me stay here rent-free and paid me for maintenance and that sort of thing. It worked out for both of us. And I got to stay close to where Debra Ellen is."

"Do you mean as a ghost?" asked Anita. "What makes you think she's still here?"

Slim chuckled. "I'm sure some people would say I'm seeing or hearing things, but now and then I'll see a light on in the house when I know there's no one there, or I hear music from upstairs where the boys' bedrooms were. It's the kind of music she liked to listen to." He jerked a shoulder. "Who or what else could it be?"

Christie shivered and wrinkled her nose. "Does your niece ever communicate with you in a direct way? I mean, like, here in your cottage, maybe."

"I don't hear voices, if that's the kind of thing you mean. But every now and then that orange tomcat comes over here and howls and meows at me like I'm supposed to understand what he's saying. I swear he's trying to tell me something." Slim smiled wistfully and looked up toward the sky. "Debra Ellen loved cats. Most of the time, that big tabby stays in the manor house and takes care of the mice. I leave him bowls of dry food and water every few days. Sometimes I see him prowling outside in the trees closer to that old fence."

"Speaking of the fence," said Christie, "do you know that there's an old hole in it big enough for humans to get through? We found it when we were looking for another way to get on the property when the gate is locked."

Slim chuckled. "You could've asked me and I would've told you about it. It's been there since my daddy was in high school, and probably before that. Even I used that break in the fence when I was a teenager to sneak up from the school to smoke."

"Why hasn't Mrs. Lindemann asked you to fix it?" Anita asked. "You mentioned having to chase ghost hunters off the property sometimes. Isn't that how they might get in?"

"Well, now, missy. First she'd have to know about it, and I haven't bothered to tell her. So far, no harm's been done by leaving it be. Most people don't know about it unless they grew up here or were told about it. And it gives me a legitimate reason to stay on the premises and chase strangers off if need be." Slim grinned broadly and leaned back deeper in his chair, his legs now crossed at the ankle.

"That's a good one, Slim," said Christie. "But did you ever consider that it may have been how your niece's killer and now Lauren's murderer were able to escape?"

Slim's smile faded. "Yes. I thought about that, but I believe whoever was guilty of Debra Ellen's murder was already here on the premises. And nobody locked the big gate to the driveway in those days, so he could've just driven away like nothing had happened."

# CHAPTER TWENTY-TWO

Jason called while Christie and Anita were driving down the hill above the town to Anita's condo.

"I have some new information from Ben," he said excitedly. "Are you free to meet me for tacos at the Silver Spoon?"

"Sounds great," said Christie. "Anita's with me. Is it a problem if she joins us?"

"Not at all. I'll grab a table and meet you there in about ten minutes."

It turned out there was a sizable crowd at the popular pub considering it was a weeknight, even for being the night for cheap tacos. The Seattle Mariners were playing on multiple screens in the big room. They'd been playing well so far in the early season, which was most likely the reason for the full bar and tables. The team's fans hoped fervently every season that *this* would be the year they get to their first World Series, but they'd been disappointed thus far.

Christie spotted Jason at a table in the farthest corner of the noisy room, directly under one of the wall-mounted TV monitors. She waved and threaded her way across the room with Anita right behind.

The gentleman that he was, Jason stood and gave Christie a quick hug and pulled out two chairs.

"Thanks for snagging a table. I'm guessing no one wanted to sit here because you'd have to have a neck like a stork to see the game," said Christie.

"Maybe that, plus I happened to get here just as the three guys sitting here got up to leave."

"Not Mariners' fans?" said Christie.

"Dodgers' fans, I'm assuming," Jason said. "One of them was wearing a baseball cap with their logo. Mariners are ahead eight to one. They couldn't stand to watch their team lose, I guess." He signaled the young lady who was weaving her way to their table with a basket of tortilla chips and salsa.

"We'll take a pitcher of Modelo and two of your special tacos with all the works for each of us, please."

"And three glasses?" She scribbled the order and winked at Jason, who nodded. The server's left arm was tattooed from wrist to shoulder with colorful images, none of which made any sense to Christie.

"What's the news?" Christie asked while reaching for chips. "I have something to tell you after you tell us what Ben discovered."

"This afternoon, I looked through the files that Detective McAvoy shared with me and had Ben take a peek at them also. There were unique details that hadn't been made public but combined with what Ben's search turned up, I think it's reasonable to consider that someone in the house was directly responsible for the death of Debra Ellen, instead of it being totally accidental."

"What makes you say that? What's your proof?"

"For one thing, the police found a girl's tennis shoe in one of the boys' bedrooms. It was definitely way too small to belong to any of the three teenage boys who wore size ten or eleven shoes. But it was explained away as belonging to a niece who had been in the house a few days earlier."

"Did they identify the niece?" Christie asked.

"If they did, there's no note to document it. But I suppose that could've been an oversight."

Gina, the server, returned with the beer and three frosted pint glasses. The threesome refrained from talking while she poured the first round.

They toasted each other and the Mariners and after the first swig, Jason continued. "There was also a question of some of the footprints that were found on the widow's walk. The lady of the house, Mrs. Donaldson, stated that no one had been up there in the several days before the incident. It had rained the day prior, so the prints were thought to be very recent. She also swore that no was home at the time when all this happened. She contended that Debra Ellen must have entered the house while the family was attending an away football game."

"How would she have gotten in if they were all gone? And were the footprints made by more than one person?" asked Anita. "Did she have a key?"

"Mrs. Donaldson guessed that one of the boys accidentally left the door unlocked, which wasn't a big deal in those days because they didn't have any neighbors within a half mile."

"You didn't answer my question about footprints," said Christie. "Did the report say how many different shoes made them?"

Jason shook his head. "It just said there were 'several sets of footprints,' but no additional detail."

The tacos arrived with sides of sour cream and guacamole. The trio devoured half of the tacos before anyone spoke again.

"What did Ben find out?" Christie asked while she licked sour cream off her fingers. "Beyond what was in the newspapers, I mean."

"I specifically asked him to track down the people who owned Langley Manor and any close friends of the three boys, who were fourteen, eighteen, and nineteen at the time. I wanted to know where they'd moved to and if there were any run-ins with the law at any other time."

"And?" Christie asked, curiosity piqued at the comment about the law.

"They moved to Olympia, where Mr. Donaldson was hired as a teacher at one of the elementary schools."

"Is that all?" Christie asked between bites. "I don't see how it helps solve Lauren's murder. Or how it's connected. Lauren wasn't pregnant, according to the autopsy."

"I'm not sure either, but it's all he's come up with so far. And maybe it's not connected at all." Jason refilled the three empty glasses. "You said you learned something. Maybe it's better than what I have."

Christie and Anita looked at each other with smug grins. Christie took a big breath. "We drove up the road to Langley Manor and parked near the gate, then we walked along the property line so we could look for an opening in the fence, like my mom told me about last Sunday. We found a place where the chain link fence had been cut open, big enough for a person to get through."

"It was mostly covered over with blackberry vines," said Anita, sliding her sleeve up to reveal some nasty-looking scratches. "It was also rusted over like it's been that way for years. Christie used loppers to cut some branches back so we could've gone through, and we considered it, but we didn't."

"That surprises me," said Jason. "Why didn't you?"

"We just wanted to see if there was another way to get onto the grounds other than via the main drive," said Christie. "I'm beginning to think that someone snuck onto the property and into the building. Perhaps someone knew Lauren was going to be there and needed to silence her."

"But what proof do you have of any of that?" Jason asked, ever the lawyer who operated on real evidence, not mere allegations.

"No proof yet, but I think Lauren was planning to confront someone at the wedding about this clipping." Christie opened the notebook and handed it to Jason, reminding him to not touch the yellowed paper.

"Anita and I got permission from the caretaker to check the house again, and I found this near the stairs. It might have slipped from Lauren's hands when she fell and then it slid under the baseboard." Closing the notebook, she continued, "I'm going to get this to McAvoy in a bit. Maybe it'll stimulate his brain cells."

Jason scanned the short article.

"Hmm. Ben should've found this bit of information as well, but he didn't say so. It does shed some light on the possibility of Debra Ellen being murdered, as the caretaker suggested to you. And a connection between the two deaths."

"And there's more."

"More what?"

In a mysterious voice, Christie said, "Slim said he's seen lights turn on in the house when he knows it's empty and that he's heard music from one of the bedrooms."

Jason scoffed. "He also admitted that trespassers can get

onto the property from that hole in the fence. Why doesn't he think that's what happened?"

"He didn't say, and I didn't ask. He mentioned the possibility of it being his niece's ghost, waiting until her murderer is found."

"Seriously? Who really believes in ghosts anyway?" Jason said as he prepared to take another swallow of beer.

Anita said, "Slim does. He even thinks the orange cat is trying to tell him something. He said Debra Ellen loved cats."

"Perhaps Slim's niece came back as a cat," teased Christie. "Debra Ellen might be hiding in plain sight."

"I just remembered something else, Christie," said Anita. "We saw Pastor Smith leaving Langley Manor when we were about to walk to the car."

"Are you sure it was him?" Jason asked. "Why would he be up there?"

"Exactly," Christie said, tipping her glass to him.

# CHAPTER TWENTY-THREE

Christie hurried through her morning routine at home. She'd hit the snooze button too many times and overslept by a half hour. McAvoy had told her when she called after tacos Wednesday evening that he couldn't meet her that night but would see her at the shop early Thursday morning. He'd had a complaint to attend to the evening before because it was Officer Newell's turn to have a free night with Chief Conway out of town.

Her aunt Doris was busy in the flower room, with her flying fingers creating corsages and boutonnières. She'd been doing this for more than forty years and had it down pat. She always made a few extra just in case someone forgot to order ahead or had a last-minute change in plans.

McAvoy showed up shortly after opening. Christie shared what she'd learned about the fence and gave him the clipping that she'd slipped into a sandwich bag for safety. "Slim—you remember, the caretaker—had the same article in a notebook that he kept from when his niece died. Can you check that out?"

"Jason came by already this morning—that's why I'm a little later than I expected—and left a summary of findings. He also mentioned that a girl's shoe was found at the house, but it was never proven who it belonged to. You know we're short-handed this week with the chief out of town, but I'll have Newell make some phone calls. Fortunately, Ben was able to get some updated phone numbers for us. Newell can check on that shoe as well, if it's still in evidence."

"I really think you should talk to Slim yourself. You might even end up believing in ghosts." Christie smiled impishly, her green Irish eyes sparkling.

"I don't know about believing in ghosts, but I'll talk to him. You might want to know that we finally caught up with the supposed boyfriend. Adam. He's a bit strange and doesn't seem concerned that he's being considered a suspect in Lauren's death. He's either a good actor or he's innocent. I don't know which yet, and I don't have any legitimate evidence to charge him. I have some names to talk to that he gave me as alibis."

"So nothing there yet, then. " Christie sighed. "You might ask him if he knows about the hole in the fence. And does he have a last name? I've never heard what it is."

McAvoy jotted down a few words. "If he knows about the fence, I wouldn't expect him to admit it, but I'll try an indirect way of asking him. His last name is Lawrence. He said he grew up in Olympia. Anything else?"

"Oh, yes. I almost forgot. Have you talked with Pastor Smith about being up at Langley Manor Tuesday evening? I know he's, like, a friend of Mrs. Elliott, and he's doing the funeral service for Lauren at the Baptist church in Elida—at least I think it's in Elida—but why would he be at the mansion?"

McAvoy looked at Christie, his lips pursed. "That's a good

question. I'd like to know the answer to that myself." He scribbled another few words, closed his ever-handy notebook, and pocketed it. "I'll make a few phone calls. Nice work, Miss Detective." He tipped his hat and hurried out the front door.

Christie grabbed an apron and joined her aunt to help with the corsages.

"What was that about you seeing the pastor at Langley Manor, young lady? What were you and Anita doing up there in the first place?" Aunt Doris glared at Christie over her half-glasses, her hazel-green eyes on fire. "There have been two murders up there already. Are you trying to be the third?"

Christie took her aunt's stern manner to be concern instead of anger. "We weren't at the manor directly, Auntie. We were checking out the fence between the condos and the mansion to see if there was still an opening that someone could use to gain access to the property. You know, like Mom said there was back when the high school was up on the hill."

"And why would you be doing that? I seem to recall that you weren't going to get more involved with this case. Hmm?"

"I wanted to check for myself. Detective McAvoy didn't tell me to do it, if that's what you're thinking, and we were never in any danger. We found the opening. The fence is overgrown with blackberry vines, but we found where it had been cut open. It was rusted over, but it's still passable if you beat down the bushes. Basically, it proves that someone could've gotten up to the manor without going through the gate, like when it's locked. And it looked like it had been used recently. There were some fresher cuts and broken stems on the vines."

Christie clipped several baby pink rosebud stems and bundled them with a few wisps of baby's breath. She added a pair of peach-toned alstroemeria blooms and looked at the corsage with a critical eye. "I think it needs a dark pink ribbon. What do you think, Auntie?"

Aunt Doris glanced at the pretty creation. "It needs some of that dark purple aster to make it pop." She handed several stems across the table. "Add a purple ribbon, and it's perfect."

"Thank you, Auntie! You're wonderful!"

"Humph. What about this Pastor Smith? You seem to be suspicious of him."

Christie tied the ribbon on the corsage and placed it carefully in its container with the order taped to the outside. "Well," she said, leaning with her hands resting on the edge of the table, "he seemed a little friendlier than I thought was proper when he was at Lauren's home. I overheard Lauren's grandmother and him call each other by their first names, which seemed odd for a professional visit to discuss funeral plans. I can't explain just why, but something about how he interacted with her made me think there was some history in the background."

"It could just be his style, or maybe she's been one of his church members for a long time and they know each other well."

Christie shook her blonde curls, her lips pinched together. "It gave me a weird feeling, that's all." She shivered involuntarily.

Doris looked up at the ceiling in exasperation. "I can ask around and see if I can find out something about him, if you like. I've got a few friends in the Baptist congregation here in White Castle. They might know if something's going on in Elida."

"That would be lovely, Auntie!" Christie blew a kiss across the table. "I mean, I don't want to accuse him of being a bad guy without more evidence, but it wouldn't be the first time that someone we're supposed to trust wasn't deserving of it after all."

"Amen to that," Aunt Doris said with an edge to her voice. "I'll call my friend Myrna when I'm done with these orders."

# CHAPTER TWENTY-FOUR

Christie sat down at her computer during a lull after the lunch hour. It was typically slow at that time of day, and she often sent her aunt out for her own lunch break after a busy morning. Earlier that day, Anita had sent her some photos of the floral decorations at Tiffany and Drew's wedding. Christie had started an album of her creations as a reference for future clients.

With her critical eye, Anita had become the unofficial photographer for the album. She'd snapped photos of the beautifully decorated pergola on the patio, the archway inside the ballroom, and the other flowers that adorned the pews. She'd also taken pictures of the tabletop arrangements, a few of which included some of the wedding party and happy guests. Christie selected several of the photos to print for the album, happy that Anita had managed to take the photos before the unfortunate event that would have wiped those smiles off everyone's faces.

Stormy sat on the counter while Christy inserted the eight

by eleven-inch prints into cellophane sleeves but jumped back to her observation post when the front door chime rang.

Christie looked up to acknowledge her customer. Her heart skipped a beat when she recognized Pastor Smith walking toward her. She stood to greet him. "Hello, Pastor Smith. How can I help you today?"

He smiled politely. "I just wanted to thank you for that nice gesture of flowers for the Elliotts. It meant a lot to Mrs. Elliott."

"You're very welcome. She seemed like a nice person, and I wanted to let her know that I cared about her granddaughter, even if I didn't know Lauren before she passed."

"Yes, Ms. O'Mara. Theresa, um, Mrs. Elliott is a good lady."

Christie noticed the use of her first name. "You seemed quite friendly with her."

The pastor said rather smoothly, "Well, you see, the Elliotts haven't lived in Elida all that long, so they haven't had a chance to get to know a lot of people. Plus, it's a small town and the long-timers are pretty close-knit—they don't take to newcomers all that easily. I took a special interest in them both, you know, to help them fit in as new parishioners."

"No 'Welcome Wagon' there?" Christie recalled her own grandmother talking about being part of the local Welcome Wagon group until it disbanded quite some years ago. Grandma Maude had always provided something flower-related. It was a nice gesture, and she saw it as inexpensive advertising of a sort.

"There were some circumstances, uh, around their arrival that made it difficult for her and her husband to assimilate into the community."

"I don't understand."

"I'll try to explain. Frank Elliott was a bank manager in Olympia. He moved to Elida because he wanted a quieter community for his wife and daughter. The home that they bought had belonged to the previous bank manager, John Thompson, who had left town unexpectedly. Some people think Mr. Elliott pulled strings to get the position in Elida and that the Thompsons were ultimately forced to sell their home quickly at a bargain price."

"As I understand it, those kinds of transfers happen regularly in the business world, whether it's a bank or a department store," said Christie, unmoved by the story.

"In a little town like Elida, that can make it really tough for the new family to fit in. Theresa has been getting the cold shoulder for three years. Thankfully, Lauren was already out of high school, so she didn't have to struggle with that. She already has a challenge with socializing due to her autism. As a matter of fact, Theresa said Lauren had only recently managed to make friends, like Jazmine, because of taking classes at the community college in Chehalis."

"What about Lauren's new job? Was that at the bank in Elida where her father was the manager?"

Pastor Smith winced. "Yeah, it was. That caused some more unhappiness because the loan officer thought his own daughter should have been hired for the position."

"Hmm. Do you know if the two girls were equally qualified?"

"There's no way for me to know for sure, but it smells of nepotism, regardless of their individual skills."

"I can understand that," said Christie.

Stormy chose that moment to hop down to the counter. She walked the few steps across the counter with her back arched and sniffed the pastor's coat sleeve. Then she sat back on her haunches and hissed at him.

Pastor Smith pulled his arm away sharply and stepped back from the counter.

Stormy retreated to her perch where she sat with her tail flicking back and forth.

"Stormy! What was that all about?" Christie scolded her kitty mildly, although she felt like hissing at the pastor herself for reasons she didn't yet understand. She asked smoothly, "Do you have an animal at home? Stormy may be reacting to the scent of another cat or a dog."

He shook his head and brushed something invisible off his sleeve. "I don't have any animals. I don't have the time or patience with my workload." He glanced at the photos and album lying open on the counter. "What are the pictures for? It seems like nobody bothers to print them up these days."

Christie turned the binder around so Pastor Smith could see them more clearly. "This is a reference album where I can show prospective clients examples of what I've done. It can be helpful for them when they're trying to decide what they want for a wedding or a party. Sometimes they bring in pages from magazines, but not always." She flipped the page to the photo she'd just inserted, showing the decorated pergola and tables on the patio at the Langley Manor. "This one is from the wedding last Saturday. It shows what I can do to make an ordinary patio into a magical place for a reception."

Christie realized too late that maybe she should have shown him a different set of photos when she saw the pastor's face blanch.

"Is that the place where Lauren was found?" he asked with a shaky voice. "That's the same day she died, you know."

"I'm so sorry," said Christie, hurriedly closing the album and sliding it and the loose photos off the counter to the shelf below. "I wasn't thinking..."

"No, that's okay. I know it wasn't intentional." He stepped back from the counter again and glared at Stormy. "Thanks again for your kindness to the Elliotts. I truly appreciate it. Good-bye now."

Aunt Doris walked in the back door as the pastor exited the front. She noticed Stormy's flicking tail and asked, "What's wrong with your cat? She seems angry or upset."

"She didn't like Pastor Smith, whatever her reason is. I don't like him much myself, but I didn't hiss at him, like Stormy did, though I was tempted," Christie said mischievously.

"Why did he come to the shop? White Castle is a good half-hour's drive from Elida."

Christie gave a little shrug. "He said he wanted to thank me for the flowers I took to the Elliotts the other day, even though he'd already thanked me. Then something curious happened. He saw the album lying on the counter with some of the pictures that Anita took at the manor last Saturday. I'd been putting them into the wedding album when he came in. He asked about them, so I explained what they were. He turned really pale and hurried out the door after saying something about Lauren having died there. I can't imagine what caused that reaction."

"I'd better talk to Myrna soon," said Aunt Doris.

# CHAPTER TWENTY-FIVE

Christie felt more tired than usual Thursday evening after what had turned out to be a busy afternoon at the shop. After enjoying one of her mother's delicious leftover meals, she sat curled up with her kitty and a glass of wine. She wasn't a regular user of social media, but a comment from Anita had triggered her memory about her plan to search Facebook regarding Lauren's death. She logged on and entered Lauren's name using the surname Elliott. She scanned the list of friends, looking for any connections she might find among the names she'd collected so far: Adam, Jazmine, Stephanie, Tiffany, and Drew.

Lauren hadn't posted very often, which didn't really surprise Christie, knowing of her introverted nature. There were no photos at all. Next, Christie typed in Jazmine's name and did the same kind of search. A slew of photos and posts popped up. Jazmine was definitely more socially adept. She went straight to the list of friends, one of which was a guy named Ethan, whom Christie hoped was the same person as Adam's friend. She did a similar search for Ethan, Stephanie,

Drew, and Tiffany. Twenty minutes later, she'd scanned enough posts and photos to be suspicious that there was some kind of connection between all of them, although she didn't find a specific common element. She wondered what it was. They'd gone to different high schools, had varied careers, and shared no obvious common interests. But they periodically showed up in pictures in one another's posts.

She called Jason and told him of her search results. "I can't put my finger on whatever it is that's bugging me about Lauren and Adam and their so-called friends. But that's not why I called. Pastor Smith came to my store today, supposedly to thank me for those flowers I took to Lauren's grandmother. And you know how Stormy seems to have some sixth sense about some people and hisses at them? Well, she clearly didn't like the pastor."

After describing the cat's reaction, she continued, "He was startled, of course, and I apologized for her while I put her back on her perch. When he saw some of the pictures that Anita had taken at the manor—I was putting them into the wedding album for my clients—he went pale and backed away like, well..." She rolled her eyes at the only expression that came to mind." Like he'd seen a ghost. He asked where they'd been taken and then sort of admonished me because he realized they were from the place Lauren died. He's doing her funeral, you know."

"Yes, but why would it bother him about the pictures? Lauren wasn't in them, was she?"

"No, at least... I don't think so. I suppose I should double-check. I'll look at the enlarged versions again when I'm at work tomorrow."

"Here's a different thought," said Jason. "Do you think he might have recognized someone else?"

"I don't know. He's from Elida, and I got the impression

that Drew's and Tiffany's friends and guests were mostly from around here. But it's certainly possible, I guess. But why would he go ghost white?"

Jason chuckled. "There's that 'ghost' word again. I might start believing in them myself if this keeps up."

"Ha, ha," said Christie. "Anyway, I talked to McAvoy earlier today, and he was going to have Officer Newell chat with Pastor Smith about his interest in Adam and his ghost blog. He also said he'd look for the tennis shoe that you said Ben discovered was found in the Debra Ellen case."

"If he finds the shoe, it could be tested for DNA. Back in the nineties, when she died, there wasn't much of that done, especially if the death was declared accidental, and even less so in small communities like White Castle."

"Good point. But don't they need some DNA to compare it to? What if the police didn't save anything personal of Debra Ellen?"

"They could check samples of any living relatives," said Jason.

"Her mother's dead," said Christie. "And her father too."

"The caretaker is her uncle. He should be a close enough match for comparison."

"You're absolutely right!" Christie suddenly felt more hopeful. "Will you mention it to the detective?"

"Of course. I have some other information he wanted anyway."

"Great. Now, back to Pastor Smith. I think this might be one of those background checks that Ben is so good at. I'm very curious about his history before he landed in Elida."

"Consider it done."

~

Christie leaned back into her grandma's chair and picked up her glass of wine. Thinking out loud, she asked Stormy, "Who is the most likely person to have wanted Lauren dead? Or was it totally an accident? No, strangling someone isn't accidental, even if her falling down the stairs was unintentional."

She took a swallow of the dark red drink. "But who strangled her? Could it have been someone from the wedding party? The doesn't seem likely because he—and I'm assuming it's a 'he,' Stormy, because of that extra set of footprints looking too big for a girl—would've had to go through the ballroom to get back out to the reception. And surely someone would've noticed. Or was everyone in the kitchen by then, or serving the guests on the patio?"

Christie thought back to the bustle that had occurred between the short but sweet wedding to the first few minutes of the reception. She recalled a semi-orderly movement of the guests through the main door of the building out to the patio. At the time, she couldn't have known that she would be trying to recreate that scene later and hadn't paid attention to every detail.

"What am I missing?" she asked herself aloud, startling Stormy, who had started purring during her silent soliloquy.

She picked up her cell and called Anita. "Do you remember when we talked about the second set of stairs that went behind the kitchen to the maid's quarters?"

"Yes, and we debated whether the maid lived on the second floor or the third floor. Why?"

"I was just thinking about how the murderer would've been seen by someone from the catering staff if he—and I'm assuming it's a he—came down the stairs from the second floor the normal way. I mean, by the stairs that the family used. And so far, nobody saw anything unusual, or they were all busy elsewhere, like in the kitchen or on the patio."

"What are you thinking, Christie?"

"What if there's a connection between the family living quarters and the maid's quarters either on the second or third floor? Someone who knew about a passageway or a door could've killed Lauren, then left the building through the maid's quarters and down the back stairs."

"We still don't know who that would be, even if it were possible."

"I bet Slim knows about another passageway."

# CHAPTER TWENTY-SIX

Christie's plan to ask Slim about a passageway was thwarted by his failure to answer the phone and no option to leave a voice message. She went to Plan B and called Stephanie, Tiffany's maid of honor, thankful that she'd entered her contact information for the wedding.

"Hi, Stephanie. This is Christie O'Mara, the floral decorator for Tiffany's wedding. Do you have a minute? I have some questions that you might be able to answer for me."

"Sure. Yeah, I remember you. The flowers were so beautiful! I'll have to call you someday if I ever get married. But what kind of questions do you have? Wouldn't you rather talk to Tiffany?"

"Yes, but she's not back from her honeymoon, I think, until this weekend. Is that right?"

"Sometime on Saturday. Drew had to be back to work by Monday for an important client. So, what's on your mind?"

"Well, I'm helping the police with some of the interviews because they're short-staffed this week. And I know you were there when the young lady was found upstairs. Did you see or hear anything or anyone on the second floor when you and the other bridesmaids and groomsmen were getting ready? Like, was there someone you didn't know up there?"

"Hmm. I definitely didn't *see* anyone, but Lindy told me she thought she heard someone talking like it came from upstairs on the third floor, where that girl was found. And as far as we knew, nobody was up there. Tiffany said it was just storage and junk up there. I told her she probably just heard someone talking in the hallway, not upstairs."

Christie felt her skin prickle. "Did she say whether it was a male voice or a female voice?"

"She didn't say, and I didn't ask," Stephanie replied. "Would you like me to call her and find out? I'd be glad to do that."

"Oh, that would be great. Thank you. You can call me at this cell number anytime."

"Sure. Since you're helping the police with this case, I suppose I can tell you something that I overheard Tiffany say, but I probably wasn't supposed to know. At least I doubt she would've told me if she hadn't had too much to drink."

"Was this at the wedding?"

"No, not then. It was two weeks ago when we had a girls' weekend at the beach. You know, the bridesmaids and a few other sorority friends and Tiffany all got together to celebrate her getting married. And all that."

"Of course. I'm sure that was a lot of fun."

"It was, except when Tiffany got a little drunk and started saying things about Drew and his father. You know, not very nice stuff. And she was getting married to him and has a two-carat emerald-and-diamond ring!"

"What do you mean? What kind of stuff?"

"This is the part I don't think she meant for us to hear, because she was talking to Drew on the phone and kinda forgot we were all there together. But she said something like, 'Why would he give someone fifty thousand dollars? Did he get her pregnant or something? Sounds like family gossip to me.' Then she started laughing and saying she loved him and all that. She seemed embarrassed when she turned around and saw us and realized we might have heard her talking."

"Did you ask her what she meant by her comments?"

"No way! We all acted like we hadn't heard anything, because we were talking so loud and listening to music and playing silly board games all at the same time."

"Do you have any idea who she might have been talking about? The girl, I mean. Or even the man involved."

"No. None."

Christie thought for a second, then asked, "Had they been engaged for a long time?"

"No, not at all. Tiffany didn't even know Drew until her father transferred his stock assets to a new company. He hired an asset manager to help, who turned out to be Drew, and Tiffany's dad encouraged Drew to meet his daughter. They started dating barely six months ago, and I guess you could say it was love at first sight. Drew's father was some kind of financial guru in another company but he told Tiffany, who told me, that Drew wanted to make his own way instead of working for his dad. I'd say he's doing well, if you can judge by that engagement ring."

"What about the rumor I heard that Drew had been engaged to someone else not long ago?"

"I'm sure it was just a rumor. I didn't know Drew before Tiffany started dating him, but I can imagine other girls wishing they were Tiffany."

"Are you one of them?"

"Of course not! I'm planning to be a nurse practitioner. I don't have time for someone like Drew right now."

"Someone like Drew?"

Stephanie scoffed into the phone. "Well, for one thing, Drew's ego is enormous. He seems to need to be the center of attention, and I think he was trying to impress other people by giving Tiffany that ginormous rock on her finger. Basically, he's just not my type of guy. Hey, there's someone at my door. If you have any other questions, give me a ring. Bye."

Christie stared at her phone for a moment after the abrupt disconnection. She was more than curious about the fifty thousand dollars that someone may have paid to an unidentified female. It was only eight o'clock, so she dialed Jason.

"Hi, beautiful," he said in greeting. "I almost called you a few minutes ago but thought I'd save it till tomorrow. But since you called, I'll tell you now."

"Tell me what?"

"McAvoy got preliminary DNA results back from that tennis shoe that was still in evidence. And from the dress that Debra Ellen was wearing when she was found. The DNA sequences are identical, which I'm sure doesn't surprise you."

"True. But that doesn't get us any closer to the killer. It just confirms what was already suspected, that someone in the house was the guilty party."

"But," said Jason, "it gives McAvoy license to pursue the Donaldsons. The positive identification proves that Debra Ellen was in the house long enough to lose a tennis shoe at some point."

"But Jason, it doesn't get us any closer to *who* killed her. Is McAvoy going to put all of them on trial? And what about the friend who was at the Donaldsons' all the time, according to the reports at the time? What evidence is he going to use now that wasn't available then?"

"He's asked Ben to keep looking for any information that

can tie this all together. Ben's very good at what he does. I'd put my money on his finding something."

"I hope so. I talked to Stephanie—she was Tiffany's maid of honor—just before I called you. I didn't get a chance to ask her if she knew Lauren or Adam, or even Ethan, for that matter. We were talking about the rumor that Drew had been engaged to someone else a short time before he met Tiffany. She said he had a huge ego when I asked if she'd been one of the women who would've liked to date him."

"It doesn't sound like she likes him very much."

"And Tiffany had mentioned someone giving fifty thousand dollars to someone, presumably a female, because she joked about getting that person pregnant."

"Did Stephanie mention who Tiffany had been talking to?"

"No. But I'll tell McAvoy about it."

# CHAPTER TWENTY-SEVEN

Mrs. Fremmerlid, Christie's high school English teacher—and recently published author of a romance novel—was the first customer through the door Friday morning. Christie met her halfway to the entrance and hugged her like an old friend.

"How are the book sales going, Mrs. Fremmerlid? Is *Twilight in Havana* on the bestseller list yet?"

"No, but all my friends have bought a copy, and that's good enough for me. I really just wanted to prove that I could write a novel."

"What are you doing next? I can't imagine that you're going to stop writing now that you've experienced how it feels."

"You're right about that. My family wants me to write a book about the adventures we had while the kids were growing up. All three of my children volunteered to pitch in with details about their favorite road trips, summer camp, fishing with their dad, and that kind of thing. I guess I could also include bits about my own early life and their dad's too. It wouldn't be so much a memoir but more like something they could pass on to their own children. And maybe grandchildren, eventually."

"That's a wonderful idea. I would've loved to know more about my own grandparents and their younger days. What a change they would've experienced when their families moved from Ireland to the United States." Christie sighed wistfully. "I didn't ask Grandma Maude enough questions when I was young."

"I'm glad you like the idea, Christie. Now, the reason I'm here is to find something for my granddaughter's bridal shower coming up next week. I'll just browse around, if you don't mind."

"Of course. Do you mind my asking where your granddaughter lives? Has she chosen a florist for the wedding?"

"Unfortunately, she lives on the other side of the state in Spokane. If she were getting married anywhere close to White Castle, you can be sure I'd recommend that she hire you."

"That's kind of you. I'll leave you alone to look for something for her while I attend to business."

Christie finished printing the orders that had come in overnight and walked them back to her aunt in the flower room. "Are you almost finished with that order for the Olsen funeral? The funeral home is sending someone to pick it up because I told them I couldn't deliver until later today."

"Working on it now, honey."

"Thanks, Auntie." Christie rang up the items that Mrs. Fremmerlid had selected. "Would you like these gift-wrapped today?"

"Yes, Christie. That would be so nice. My fingers aren't as nimble as they used to be."

Christie tucked the figurine and a pair of wine glasses into a white box and then wrapped it in bridal-shower-appropriate paper. She'd found beautiful paper at a gift show earlier in the year that added a special touch of elegance to each wrapped package.

"That's gorgeous, Christie. Very classy."

Christie beamed at her teacher's compliment. "Thank you. I personally think the wrapping is almost as important as the gift inside. I'm sure your granddaughter will enjoy your gifts. I know I would like them."

The shop phone rang almost simultaneously with the front door chime, signaling the entrance of a customer.

"I'll take the phone, Christie," Aunt Doris called from the flower room in the back.

Christie watched as a young man with longish hair walked slowly across the front part of the shop, his eyes darting right and left as he approached the order desk. He wore low-slung jeans and a T-shirt with long sleeves that peeked out from the cuffs of a black-and-cream plaid jacket.

"Are you Christie?" he asked.

"Yes. How can I help you?" Christie's heart palpitated for a moment. She recognized the face from her Facebook search, but she didn't recall which of the young men it belonged to. A second later, she realized it was the man in the photo with Lauren on her computer.

"You've been asking around about me. I'm Adam Lawrence. Lauren was one of my friends."

Christie's hands felt moist. She wished she had one of those buttons that called the police when a robbery was happening, even if she didn't think that was why Adam was there.

"Hello, Adam. Yes, I've been wanting to meet you. How can I help you today?"

"Jazmine—you know, one of Lauren's friends—has been bugging me to talk to you, but I lost the number she gave me.

Then I remembered her saying something about a florist and that wedding up at the mansion. Since this is the only flower shop in White Castle, I figured this had to be the right one."

Christie nodded. "Yes, I'm the only game in town." She wanted to talk with him about talking with McAvoy but was afraid he would turn and run out the door. She sent a mental message to McAvoy but didn't expect him to get it. She considered reaching for her cell but decided it was too risky. She wanted to find out more from Adam before he left.

Stormy hopped down from her perch and landed next to Christie.

Adam reached out with his palm up and let the kitty sniff at his fingers. "I think your cat likes me," he said with a smile.

Christie groaned inwardly. She didn't want Stormy to like Adam.

"Were you with Lauren last Saturday at Langley Manor?" she finally managed to ask, although she didn't know how she would be able to tell if he answered truthfully or not.

A long moment passed while Adam stroked Stormy's chin and nuzzled her face while Stormy purred.

Christie thought to herself, *Traitor! Why are you being nice to him?*

She looked up when the front door chimed the entrance of a customer. Adam turned his head quickly to see who it was. Christie felt her heart settle down when she saw that it was McAvoy. He nodded toward her aunt—she must have sent him a message on her cell phone.

Christie sensed a change in Adam's demeanor as soon as he noticed that McAvoy was a cop. But he didn't run out the door as she expected him to. Instead, Adam extended his hand to the detective and said, "I'm Adam Lawrence, Officer. I heard you're looking for me."

# CHAPTER TWENTY-EIGHT

McAvoy leaned against the counter on an elbow. "Adam Lawrence? Yes, I have a few questions for you, if you have time."

"Certainly, Officer."

"Actually, it's Detective McAvoy... Christie, may I borrow your consultation area for a few minutes?" McAvoy jerked his head toward the desk in the back of the store.

"Of course," she replied. "I'll turn on some music so your conversation will be more private."

Christie slipped in a CD of Muzio Clementi's sonatas. The pleasant sounds created a calming background for working and shopping in addition to obscuring McAvoy's interrogation. It crossed her mind that the detective could have taken Adam down to the police station, which was only a few blocks away. The least she could do was provide some sense of privacy.

Donning her work apron, she joined her aunt in the flower room. The undulating hum of the flower cooler further blunted the voices from around the corner. She knew that giving them that privacy was appropriate, but she ached to know what was being said. So, she tried her best to concentrate on her work.

"Auntie, how many orders do we still have to finish for the funeral this afternoon?"

Aunt Doris held up five fingers. "Fred Bishop is going to be here before noon to pick them up. I told him Heather couldn't deliver until after school, and that would be too late."

"That's nice of him to offer." Christie pulled the next order from the clipboard and selected a vase and the flowers she planned to use. "I'd love to be a little bug in there with McAvoy and Adam," she said quietly. "That's the so-called boyfriend of the girl who died last weekend. I wonder why he came here."

"I sensed trouble when I heard him say his name," whispered her aunt.

"Thank you for alerting McAvoy. I didn't know you knew his number."

Aunt Doris cocked her head. "He gave it to me last year when you were kidnapped so I could text him in case I heard from you before he found you."

"It came in handy today. Thank you." Christie blew a little kiss across the table to her beaming aunt.

"Hey, Christie," said McAvoy, poking his head into the workroom. "Mr. Lawrence and I are going to go down to the station after all. Thanks for letting me use your office."

"Anytime, Detective."

Christie heaved a sigh once the two men were out the door. "Drat. I was hoping McAvoy could tell me what they talked about."

"You know that would be privileged information," admonished her aunt. "He'll tell you soon enough when he can."

"Yeah. I know. But I want to know *now*!"

Christie glanced at the screen when her cell buzzed on the counter. "It's Jason. Maybe he knows something." She quickly wiped her hands on a towel and pressed the green phone icon. "Hi, Jason. Do you have some news?"

"Some, but I'm not sure it fills in the blanks yet. Ben searched public records for ownership of Langley Manor going back to when Debra Ellen died."

"I thought we already knew it was the Donaldsons, and they sold to Norma Lindemann."

"Yes, but there's more to it than that. She's related to the Donaldsons, who owned it at the time. Charles Donaldson was her younger brother."

"That *is* interesting," replied Christie. "Do you know if McAvoy interviewed her already? Did she divulge that relationship?"

"I talked to him first thing today. He said she's on his list, or more correctly on Officer Newell's list. They're still contacting people on the guest list as more likely to be helpful than the owner of the venue. This could shed a new light on things."

"McAvoy was here a few minutes ago. Adam showed up at my store—I didn't know it was him for sure until he told me—and Aunt Doris texted the detective to let him know. They just left to go to the police station."

"Did Adam tell you why he was there?"

"Not exactly, but he said he'd heard I wanted to talk to him. McAvoy showed up before he told me anything more than his name. They talked here for a few minutes before heading out. Do you think McAvoy will take his fingerprints or ask him to do a DNA swab?"

"That would be a good bet."

"I'm still focused on Adam and Pastor Smith," said Christie. "That's where I'd place my money if I was betting."

"Absolutely. Talk later."

Christie and her aunt finished the funeral flower orders by

the noon deadline. The hour between noon and one was typically busy as customers often came in during their lunch hour to pick up cards or to browse. One woman called in to schedule a consultation with Anita and Christie for a landscaping project at her newly purchased home.

The unsolved murder weighed on Christie's mind while she rang up the purchases. She was beyond curious about how McAvoy's interview with Adam was going and almost called him, but she resisted. She called Slim instead, hoping he would answer his phone this time.

"Hey, Slim. Christie from the Flower Shoppe here. Do you suppose you would show me how to get up to the maid's quarters at Langley Manor? I have this theory."

# CHAPTER TWENTY-NINE

It was late afternoon before McAvoy called. Christie asked her aunt to cover the sales counter for a few minutes and moved to the back of the shop, where it was quieter for a conversation. Moms and teenage boys had started to come to pick up the corsages and boutonnières for the dance.

"Hey, McAvoy. What did you learn?"

"I asked Adam about the ghost blog and his relationship with Pastor Smith. It sounds pretty straightforward. He'd asked Mrs. Lindemann if he could do a piece on his blog about her mansion and she was excited about it, he said. She was hoping it might give her some exposure and stir up some business. I guess there's a lot of interest in haunted buildings and mansions. Anyway, she took him on a tour and told him about some of the incidents that she couldn't explain."

"Like what?"

"She told him that she'd heard music a few times when the house was empty. And she'd felt something brush against her arm."

Christie scoffed. "She could be feeding him a bunch of hogwash. That stuff's hard to prove."

McAvoy chuckled. "Maybe so, but I'm told there are a lot of people out there who believe in ghosts."

"What about Pastor Smith? How does he figure into the picture?"

"He's apparently been following Adam's blog. Adam had posted something about hoping to investigate several haunted houses in White Castle. Pastor Smith contacted him about getting a personal tour of Langley Manor because Adam had connections with the owner."

"Why would he want to do that? I didn't think religious-type people would be likely to believe in ghosts."

"All kinds of people are superstitious, which is where I think ghosts come in."

"Okay. I'll agree with that. Back to Adam. Is he still on your suspect list? Did he tell you whether or not he was at the wedding, or if he'd seen Lauren that day?"

"He said he didn't go to the wedding. He admitted that he'd talked with Lauren earlier but was evasive about seeing her on Saturday."

"He could've been lying about not going to the wedding," said Christie.

"I agree. For now, Adam's still at the top of my list, but I don't have enough evidence to charge him with anything. I can't even prove that he was with Lauren that day. Mrs. Elliott didn't actually see him at her home. She only knew what Lauren had told her."

"Which may have been a lie if she knew they were going to the wedding at the mansion, although I don't understand why she would lie about that. But isn't it possible that she didn't know where Adam was planning to take her? Did you ever check to see if there was a wedding at the Lutheran church that same day?"

"Good point. I'll call the church and ask. Thanks for the suggestion."

~

BUSINESS DONE FOR THE DAY, and after feeding Stormy at home, Christie drove to Anita's condo to meet her.

During the short drive to Langley Manor, Anita said, "You didn't explain why we're meeting Slim. Does he have more information?"

"No, or at least not that I know of. I asked him to show me how to get up to the maid's quarters in the mansion.

"Because...?"

"Because I want to see if there's a connection or passageway between those rooms and the rest of the house without having to go back outside."

"You mean like a secret door or something?"

"Exactly!"

The gate was open when Christie reached the entrance to the driveway. She wondered if it was remotely controlled, and if it had been installed before or after Debra Ellen's murder. And if Slim would know.

Slim waited at the foot of the grand stairs going up to the main entrance while Christie parked.

"Come on around this way," he said, pointing toward the patio. "The back entrance is around the corner." He led the way across the flagstone surface, past the kitchen door, and around a short laurel hedge, which camouflaged the far corner of the house from the patio. He produced a keyring and selected a key that he inserted into the old-fashioned door knob. He tugged on the door to get it open and reached inside to flip a switch on the wall.

Christie and Anita followed Slim up the narrow staircase. A naked light bulb shone dimly above them. A few cobwebs glistened in the light.

"Does anyone use this doorway nowadays?" Christie asked as a shiver raced up her spine.

"Not really," said Slim. "There hasn't been a maid on the premises for years. The Donaldsons used the second level for storage, I think. Mrs. Lindemann had everything that was in here hauled out when she bought the place."

They found an empty room at the top of the stairs.

"This certainly looks like a storage area," said Christie, gazing around the large room.

"There's another level upstairs, where the maid would have lived," said Slim. He opened a door on the other side of the room and slipped up the stairs after pulling a long cord to turn on the ceiling light.

"Definitely looks like the maid's quarters," said Christie.

It was empty but had clearly been built as a living space with a small sitting room, a tiny bedroom, and a minuscule bathroom with a toilet, tub, and vintage sink.

"This is pretty barren," commented Anita.

"I think it's smaller than my dorm room was at university," said Christie.

"But it's adequate," said Anita, "when you consider that the maid would've spent most of her time in the main house, and probably just slept here."

"Except there's no kitchen," said Christie. "Would she have to go down the stairs and come back in from outside for something to eat?"

"No," said Slim. "There's another door in the bedroom that connects to the main house. That's how she would enter to do her work." He crossed the room to an almost invisible door that simply slid to the right on rails.

"It's like a barn door!" Anita exclaimed. "Those are really popular in those fixer-upper shows on television these days."

"Where does it go?" Christie had crossed the room and was right behind Slim. She peered into the darkness and recognized that she was standing in the hallway where they'd found the young victim. The stairwell down to the second floor was immediately to her left.

"Were the bedrooms on the second floor when the Donaldsons lived here?" Christie asked, her heart pounding a little harder.

"Yes," said Slim. "Mr. Donaldson had his office there as well, and the boys all slept here on this floor."

Christie noticed several doors to bedrooms that she hadn't observed on Saturday in all the excitement.

She turned back to the door they'd just come through and slid it closed. "Hmm. It's hard to tell it's even there unless it's open." She examined it more closely. "There's no knob and no way to lock it from this side." She took a few steps down the hallway toward the stairway that led down to the main level. "So the maid would come through this passageway, walk down this hall, and then go down two levels of stairs to the main floor."

She paused. "I just thought of something. Someone could've come in the back way and closed the window."

"What window?"

"The window in the room where we heard the thunk and the window was open, so I closed it when Anita and I left the room, but then it was open the next day when we were giving Jason a tour."

"But why does it matter?" asked Slim.

"And how would you prove who did it?" Anita asked.

"It would suggest that there *was* someone up here prior to the wedding. I would imagine this area isn't used on a regular basis, if ever. Do you suppose Lauren or Adam might have closed it?"

"It's a possibility," said Anita. "If it was Adam that the wait staff saw walking across the lawn, he could've been up here, then used the maid's quarters to leave without being seen if he was sneaky enough."

"The connecting door may have been handy," said Christie. "Very handy."

## CHAPTER
# THIRTY

"What did you mean when you said that door was 'very handy'?" Anita asked on their way back to her condo.

"I've been trying to figure out how two murderers managed to get out of the house without being seen by anyone. It made me wonder if there was a secret passageway of some kind. Then I remembered something about a back way to the maid's quarters, and I wanted to see if my theory was correct."

"What theory?"

"It bothered me that both times when a young lady died on the widow's walk, nobody saw anything. The first time, if we're to believe Mrs. Donaldson, nobody was home and they found Debra Ellen already dead. So, in theory, no one was there to see anything, but I'm not confident Mrs. Donaldson was being truthful. She could've been protecting one of her sons."

"She also said that someone may have left the door unlocked and that's how she got in," Anita reminded her. "Do you think all the Donaldsons would've known about the maid's entrance?"

Christie said, "I wouldn't be surprised. Those boys probably explored and knew every nook and cranny of the house. They might have even used those back stairs to smuggle in girlfriends, for all we know."

Anita shot a knowing look at her friend.

"If you think about it, we all heard Lauren's scream, but we didn't see anyone running away from the scene. It seems like we or the catering staff should've seen someone shortly thereafter. So where did they go?"

"Are you theorizing that the murderer escaped through the maid's quarters?"

"Exactly. It would explain the second murder, although it may not have been necessary for the first one."

"There's a problem with your theory, Miss Detective," said Anita. "It assumes that the murderer knew about the maid's quarters."

"True, but what's the problem with my theory?"

"It implicates someone with intimate knowledge of the mansion."

"You mean like Slim?" Christie shook her head. "I don't think it's him."

"Did you notice that he wasn't limping today?"

Christie thought for a moment. "You're right. He wasn't. But maybe his leg only bothers him some of the time, like when it's cold. You know, like rheumatism."

"It wasn't any colder last week at the wedding when you said you saw him limping."

"We also have Adam," said Christie with a shrug. "McAvoy told me earlier that he was given a tour by Mrs. Lindemann when he told her about wanting to feature Langley Manor in a ghost blog. She may have shown him other ways to get in and out of the building."

"Joe—I mean, Detective McAvoy—is still interviewing some of the wedding party and guests. And there's still Oliver, of the catering crew, the only witness who said he saw anyone running off. By the way, did Adam have an alibi?"

"You know, McAvoy didn't say exactly. He did say he'd check to see if there really was another wedding that day at the Lutheran church."

"So, Adam's still on the list."

"Yes," said Christie. "Oh, drat! I forgot to ask Slim if he used a remote control to open and close the gate."

JASON WAS WAITING at Christie's house when she arrived shortly thereafter.

"Come on in, Jason," she said cheerfully. "I have a theory to share with you before we go out for dinner."

Over a glass of pinot grigio, Christie shared her thoughts about her tour at the manor and how the murderer may have gotten away.

"Interesting. And it could be the answer," Jason said. "But it doesn't lead us to the 'who.' By the way, Ben hasn't learned anything more about the Donaldson boys that's helpful. He looked at Adam's ghost blog and read old posts going back a few months. There are several claims by Adam about meeting ghosts and that boast about being able to prove they exist."

"What about Pastor Smith? I was hoping Ben could find some dirt on him."

"He's a minister, Christie, and he deserves our respect, but Ben did come up with something interesting. It may not be very helpful, but Pastor James J. Smith seems to have emerged from thin air about twenty years ago."

"What do you mean?"

"Ben was unable to find any documents that verify him as a person until he entered the ministry in 2002."

"Huh? How can he not have existed prior to that?"

"Ben said he couldn't verify him through name, address, or even social security number as having been a person prior to that time."

"Could he be one of those people in a witness protection program or something?"

"It doesn't seem very likely, but I presume it's a possibility. Ben said he'd try a different approach and dig deeper. If he *is* in one of those protection programs, Ben will probably hit a wall. Witnesses are very well protected, even with access to the dark web."

"What about his interest in ghosts? Did Ben find anything on that?"

"It appears that his interest in ghosts didn't surface until seven or eight months ago, when he suddenly started showing up on blogs, including Adam's ghost show."

"I wonder if he has any other connection besides ghosts to the mansion, because Anita and I definitely saw him leaving the other day. Someone must have let him in or out unless he has a way to open that locked gate. I doubt it was a ghost."

"Of course it wouldn't be."

"You said Ben didn't have anything helpful about the Donaldson boys. Slim said that the family moved to Olympia after Debra Ellen died. Is that where they all live now?"

"As I recall, the parents, Charles and Sarah, are still living in Lacey. Charles is a retired teacher. The boys—now adults, of course—are scattered. Alex was the oldest of the three. He became a math teacher and is in Poulsbo. Daniel, the middle boy, is a financial consultant in Tacoma. The youngest, Samuel, went into the army after high school and spent twenty years in the service. He's now in Fresno, working as a military recruiter."

"Okay. What about the 'friend' who spent a lot of time at the house? Do you know anything about him?"

"Well, now, he's an enigma. The news articles at the time reported that there were several friends who spent time at the house, but the focus was on one in particular. His name was Jeremy, and he was interviewed two or three days later. He had an alibi for the evening and there wasn't any evidence that could be linked directly to him. End of story and end of the trail. Ben couldn't find any current information on him."

"It's too bad we didn't have as much social media back then. It's harder for people to totally disappear these days."

## CHAPTER
# THIRTY-ONE

"Good morning, Auntie!" Christie called as she lifted Stormy to her perch. Joining her aunt Doris in the flower room, she asked, "Did you ever find out more about Pastor Smith from your friend?"

"Oh, yes. I'm sorry I forgot to tell you! As it happens, I saw her at the grocery store earlier this week and asked. She wasn't sure at the time, but she called me last night. She told me that he'd been in Idaho before he was invited here."

"What do you mean that he was 'invited'?"

"I don't know exactly because I'm not Baptist, but I remember talking with her about the church forming some kind of search committee. That was a few months ago at our sewing luncheon, and I didn't pay attention to details. Do you want me to find out more?"

"No, that's okay. I was just curious about his background."

Christie checked the computer for new orders. Her aunt still claimed to be mystified about how to retrieve them and didn't want to learn. She was quite happy to limit her technology skills to taking money and printing a receipt. Thankful that there were only two requests for floral bouquets that needed to be done that morning, she turned her attention to Lauren and the questions that still needed answers.

Why did Lauren have the newspaper article—if it *had* been in her hands when she fell—that Christie retrieved from the mansion? Did she get it from Adam? Did Adam have a connection to the Donaldson family? Did Lauren find it on her own when she was searching the newspaper archives? She decided to ask Adam first, and go from there if he didn't know about it.

He answered after three rings, his voice groggy.

"Hi, Adam. This is Christie from the flower shop. I hope I didn't wake you up, but I have a question that's bugging me."

"Yeah, I had a ghost-watching party at the Matson House last night. We were testing some new video equipment I found on the internet."

"Do you really think you can capture ghosts on film?" Christie held back a snicker. The house Adam mentioned had long been thought to be haunted by the ghost of the woman who had been jilted by her lover as a wealthy young lady. Her grandma Maude had told her about knowing Miss Matson, who had never married, as an eccentric but pleasant lady.

"There's some brand-new technology that just hit the market that detects cold particles. It's like the opposite of infra-red imaging."

"Sounds interesting. Were you successful?"

"Not yet, but I'm going to keep trying. So, why did you call? I doubt it was about my ghost blog."

"It's about your friend Lauren. I found a clipping at Langley Manor that she might have been holding in her hand when she fell. Do you know where she got it?"

"What kind of clipping are you talking about? I don't know anything about it. I wasn't with her the day she died—at least not then."

Christie caught her breath. "Does that mean you saw her earlier in the day?"

"Sort of. I wasn't with her, but I talked to her. She was going to go to some wedding of an old friend."

"Do you know anything about a padlock at the manor?"

"Geez! What is this? Twenty questions? I didn't talk to her about a padlock, if that's what you mean."

"What kind of car do you drive, Adam. Is it a silver SUV?"

"No, it's a black KIA. Why?"

"Just curious. What about the family that owned the manor twenty-five years ago—the Donaldsons? Did you know them?"

"How could I? I wasn't even born twenty-five years ago!" He said huffily, "I only know what I've read on the internet about how some people believe the building is haunted by the girl who died there a long time ago. That's why I've been interested in it myself. Pastor Smith too. He told me some stuff about it."

"How does he know anything about it?"

"Same as me, I guess. I never asked. You'll have to ask him yourself. Hey, lady, I gotta get going. I have a deadline to meet for my boss. Good luck finding your answers."

Christie suspected that Adam hadn't told her the whole truth, except maybe about having a deadline. The texts about the padlock had come from Adam. He fit the physical description of the young man driving the SUV, and he could have been lying about the car he drove. Or maybe the KIA was a company car? But which company?

One of the online orders was a "Thinking of You" bouquet for Drew's parents that was to be delivered that day. Glancing at the clock, Christie wondered if Drew and Tiffany were back from their honeymoon yet. Leaving her aunt to manage the last-minute pickups of the prom orders, she packed the vase for delivery and headed to Drew's parents' home near the White Castle Country Club.

The Simpson home was on a large lot that sat back from the street with a long, curved driveway. Christie admired the landscaping, which appeared to have been professionally done. She hoped to get more commissions for her garden design business and took mental notes for future reference.

Mrs. Simpson opened the door promptly.

"Hello, Mrs. Simpson. I have flowers for you from Christie's Flower Shoppe." Christie started to hand the box to Mrs. Simpson but was waved inside instead.

"Flowers! How lovely! Thank you, Miss O'Mara."

"Of course."

"The decorations for Drew and Tiffany's wedding were beautiful, as I'm sure you've been told already. It's too bad that something terrible had to happen to shorten the reception, but of course, those things happen."

"Yes, they do, unfortunately. I'm sorry for that. Did you know the girl who died?"

"No, I don't believe so. She wasn't on the guest list from my side of the family. Maybe Tiffany's mother knew her. Why?"

Christie set the flowers on the foyer table. "I was wondering because she had an invitation, so I assumed she was a guest. I'm sure Detective McAvoy has already asked Tiffany's mother." She reached for the doorknob. "I hope you enjoy your flowers."

"I will. But who are they from?" She read the small card on the plastic holder. "Uncle Charles and Aunt Sarah. That's so sweet. I'll have to give them a call. Thank you, Miss O'Mara." She smiled and closed the door

Christie practically sprinted to her car. First, she called Aunt Doris and confirmed her suspicion. Then she dialed McAvoy. Four rings and she got voice mail. Why didn't he pick up? She left a simple message to call her back soon. She was halfway back to her store when he called.

"Yes, Christie. What is it?"

"I just delivered flowers to the Simpsons, Drew's parents. The card was signed 'Love, Uncle C and Aunt S.' Guess who they are?"

"Just tell me. I don't want to play twenty questions today. It's been a week, and I still haven't solved that young lady's murder."

"I'm sure it's Charles and Sarah Donaldson who owned Langley Manor before Norma Lindemann bought it. Maybe this is the link that will connect the two murders to each other."

# CHAPTER THIRTY-TWO

Christie waited impatiently an extra five minutes after her Saturday two o'clock closing time for a young man to pick up the final corsage. He'd called and asked her if she could stay open a little longer because he had a Saturday job and couldn't get there in time. She didn't want his disappointed date on her conscience.

"Thanks, Ms. O'Mara," he said when he paid for the corsage. "This is real nice. Hey, is it true what everyone at school is saying about some girl dying because of ghosts at Langley Manor?"

Christie scoffed. "No, that wouldn't be correct. She didn't die because of ghosts. What else have you heard about it?"

"Some of the guys said that the old man who lives up there thinks his niece or something is a ghost. That's pretty weird."

Christie smiled kindly. "Don't spread rumors. I don't believe in ghosts. Have fun tonight."

Jason waited in his car until Christie waved him in after the young man left and locked the door.

"You sounded excited when you called. What is it?"

Christie told him about the flower delivery. "I already told McAvoy that I believe 'Uncle Charles and Aunt Sarah' are the Donaldsons from twenty-five years ago."

"Ben could probably find out faster than using any other search records. I'll text him in a few minutes. Thinking out loud here, one of Drew's parents could be a niece or nephew of Charles or Sarah."

Christie added, "Which means that one of Drew's grandparents is a sibling to the Donaldsons." She shook her head and laughed. "I always had trouble figuring out those genetic codes in science!"

"This isn't like Mendelian genetics, Christie. This is simply working out a family tree."

"When I talked with McAvoy, I got the impression that he'd be getting right on the family connection, assuming I'm correct about the names."

"That still doesn't prove any direct connection to Lauren's murder, although it could allow further investigation into Debra Ellen's death. I'll talk to Chief Conway on Monday when he's back in the office and offer to help with that petition to reopen the case."

"That would be so kind of you, Jason." Christie gave his hand a squeeze. "Slim will be thrilled, especially if the murderer is identified."

"No promises, of course."

"I know. I've been thinking more about the friend of the Donaldson boys and how he vanished into thin air. You told me that Pastor Smith seemed to have appeared out of thin air. It makes me think of ghosts, but I can't make any sense of how they could be connected."

"You know I don't believe in ghosts," said Jason.

Christie chuckled. "Well, speaking of Pastor Smith again, I wonder why he was up at Langley Manor. Was he looking for that ghost Adam talked about? Or for some other reason?"

"I suppose he could've had some business with Mrs. Lindemann, like doing a wedding or something," Jason suggested.

"I thought the engaged couple did that kind of thing." Christie wrinkled her forehead in thought. "Okay. This is almost the same topic, but different people. Do you know if McAvoy and Newell finished interviewing the wedding party and all the guests?"

"I doubt they would've interviewed every single person, but I'm pretty sure they were able to talk to all the primary witnesses."

"Like, who would you consider in that category?"

"Drew and Tiffany, the bridesmaids and groomsmen, the parents, wait staff, and a few others."

"That leaves out a lot of people who were there," said Christie. "I wonder if they talked to Uncle Charles and Aunt Sarah, assuming they attended, which I'd think they did, considering the flowers they sent afterward. On second thought, I'll answer my own question—I'm sure they didn't interview them because they wouldn't have known who they were yet and that they may well be related to the groom."

"They wouldn't have had any reason to even consider them as persons of interest, Christie. You haven't convinced me yet that they're significant to Lauren's death either. And Charles was cleared in the Debra Ellen incident, according to Ben."

Christie shrugged. "That doesn't mean he wasn't guilty. Or that he didn't know who was."

"That could be correct, but there isn't anything even now that would give McAvoy cause to interview them in Lauren's case."

"Unless we find out that they're related to Drew, who was supposedly engaged to Lauren at one time."

"Hmm. Someone related to someone who used to be engaged to someone who died is a suspect? That is stretching it, I think. And their engagement hasn't even been proven, Christie."

Christie scowled. "You attorneys get all hung up on technicalities."

Jason raised his palms. "Well, we have to deal with the law, and that requires due diligence and evidence. Not gut feelings and assumptions."

"Yeah, yeah, yeah." Christie crossed her arms. "Will you let me know if Ben finds out the family connection?"

"Sure, Christie. Do you have anything else planned for the rest of this afternoon? Do you want to take a drive up to Mt. St. Helens? It's a beautiful day to go there. We could pick up some food along the way and have a picnic with a view of the mountain."

Christie smiled sincerely. "That's a really sweet idea, Jason, but I need to check some things out. Can I have a rain check?"

"Of course. Are your parents expecting us for dinner tomorrow evening?"

"Yes, as usual. But Mom said next week she has to cancel for some kind of function related to my dad's job. Is that okay?"

"Sure. I love your mother's cooking anytime. I'll pick you up at five."

Christie would have loved to take Jason up on his invitation, but there were more pressing items on her to-do list. She called Anita, hoping she wasn't busy with grading papers or other such teacherly tasks.

"I'd be happy to help you with that," said Anita. "Have you cleared it with McAvoy yet?"

"No, but I don't think he'd object to me delivering flowers to the newlyweds as a friendly gesture," said Christie.

"It's not the flowers he would object to, Christie. I'm betting you're going to try to get more information out of them about Lauren's murder."

"Not exactly about the murder, but about some of the guests."

"Like who?"

"Earlier today, I delivered flowers to Drew's mother with a gift card that read 'Love, Uncle C and Aunt S.' She called them Charles and Sarah when she read it. That's the same first names as the Donaldsons who owned Langley Manor when Debra Ellen died. They've got to be connected."

"There are lots of Charleses and Sarahs in the world, Christie. Donaldsons too. It's probably just a coincidence."

"Well, I'm going to find out when we deliver the flowers that I'm going to put together at the store in a few minutes. I'll pick you up in half an hour."

# CHAPTER
# THIRTY-THREE

Saturday...

Using her ingenuity and a telephone app, Christie tracked down an address for Drew and Tiffany in a new development just outside the city limits. Anita did the navigation while Christie drove. The two-story homes were lined up like the green and red houses in a Monopoly game. The front yards were small, the houses very close together.

"These don't seem like the kind of home a successful businessman would choose for himself," said Christie. "I was imagining a home more like those near the country club."

"Drew is just getting started with his career. This may be what fits his current financial status," said Anita, "but I agree that they seem very cookie-cutter considering what we know about Tiffany and her tastes from the wedding planning."

"3501 Whispering Pines. Here it is," said Christie. "Let's do this."

"What are you going to say when she asks why you're giving her these flowers? Are you going to make up one of your wild excuses?"

"No, of course not! I'm thanking her for her business and asking that she keep Christie's Flower Shoppe in mind when she's ordering flowers later."

"And don't forget to tell her about our garden design company," said Anita. "Although I don't see much of an opportunity at this house."

Tiffany answered the door with her cell phone at her ear. "Oh. It's you. I'll finish this call and be right back." She closed the door without inviting them in.

"This is awkward," said Anita. "Do you think she wants us to go away?"

Christie shook her head. "Her house might not be ready for company yet."

The door opened a moment later, and Tiffany greeted them with more animation. "Sorry about that. I had to say goodbye to my mother, and it sometimes takes a few minutes before she gets the hint that I really need to get off the phone."

Christie held out the vase of colorful flowers. "These are for you and Drew. I want to welcome you home and thank you for asking me to do your wedding flowers."

"Well, thank you. That's very thoughtful. Would you like to come in? We're still just getting settled in and the house is a mess, but the living room is suitable for guests." She put the vase on a side table and led the way to a small sitting area. The decor was modern and spare. The few furniture pieces looked new.

"This is very nice," said Anita. "You have the taste of a designer."

Tiffany picked up a flute of champagne that was on the table in front of her loveseat. "Can I offer you a glass of something? The champagne is chilled. It's left over from the reception. It got cut short, you know."

"No thanks," said Christie. Anita crossed her fingers in an

'X' in front of her so only Christie could see it. "We don't plan to stay long."

"I notice you don't have much landscaping in front," said Anita. She reached into her purse and produced a business card that she handed to Tiffany. "We have a small garden design sideline, if you want to spruce it up sometime."

Tiffany took the card without looking at it and sat down. "Oh, this is just a temporary home until Drew makes bigger commissions. I'm not planning to stay here more than a year or two. But thank you. Please have a seat." She sat back and crossed her legs while indicating two side chairs on the other side of the coffee table. "Did the detective find out anything more about the young lady at Langley Manor? Did you know he had the audacity to keep us here an extra day for his interviews?" Her free leg pumped nervously back and forth.

"That must have been annoying," said Christie. "I hope it didn't interfere with any of your flight plans. I overheard one of the bridesmaids say something about Hawaii."

"Fortunately, our reservations were later in the day so it worked out, but Drew was really bent out of shape over it. He's okay now. Lying in the sun with no business responsibilities does wonders for one's attitude." She took a sip of champagne and smiled broadly.

"There seemed to be a lot of relatives present at the wedding," said Christie. "Do you and Drew come from large families?"

"We each have a pair of siblings and the usual aunts and uncles and cousins. I think they really came to see the haunted mansion." Tiffany giggled and swallowed more champagne.

"So you knew that another death occurred at Langley Manor about twenty-five years ago?" Christie asked. "It also involved a young woman."

Tiffany's face went blank for a second or two, then she

recovered and smiled. "No. I mean, I'd heard it was haunted, sure, but that detail wasn't mentioned when we talked to Mrs. Lindemann about using the manor for the wedding. But what relevance does it have now?"

"Maybe nothing," said Christie nonchalantly. "I wondered if that was the reason the building is said to be haunted now. It would make sense, if you think about it."

Anita stood and said in a theatrical voice as she walked around, "Just imagine Debra Ellen's ghost floating through the building, waiting for her murderer to be caught. She can't leave to join her poor mother and father as long as the case remains unsolved."

Tiffany wrapped her arms around herself. "That gives me the willies. You mean the murderer was never found?"

Christie nodded. "The police weren't able to prove who killed her at the time. But Detective McAvoy is looking into the old evidence. Maybe he'll get lucky and come up with a new suspect."

"But what does that have to do with now?" Tiffany asked after another sip of champagne. "Are you sure you don't want any?" She poured herself another glassful from the bottle sitting on the coffee table. "It's still cold." She held the bottle in the air as if that would prove its temperature.

Christie and Anita shook their heads.

"We need to get going. Anita has an appointment with a client and we've taken up enough of your time." Christie headed to the door with Anita in tow. "Thanks for your time. And congratulations to the two of you."

Tiffany reached the door in time to politely see them out and closed the door behind them.

Back in the car, Anita said, "That was clever of you to throw in that line of conversation about Debra Ellen. I have a feeling that Tiffany is the type who will say something to other family members about that unsolved murder. It just might spur someone to do or say something stupid."

"Yes. Especially one of Drew's relatives, if what would be his great-uncle Charles is the same Charles who lived at Langley Manor when Debra Ellen died."

"Do you think he's the murderer?"

"Not necessarily, but I'm sure he knows something that he didn't tell the police twenty-five years ago. So if they are the same people, at least I've found them for McAvoy. There were the three boys in the house also, his sons, whom he would want to protect."

"*If* he's the same person," Anita reminded her.

Christie puzzled through different ideas that floated through her brain as she drove back to Anita's condo. Even if Drew was related to the Donaldsons, what did that prove or even imply?

Another possibility was that the terms "Uncle" and "Aunt" could be just affectionate names for friends to a family, with no blood relationship at all. When she was a little girl, she had an "Aunt Cora," who was one of her mom's friends. Grandma Maude had explained when she was old enough to understand that Cora had never had children of her own, nor did she have any siblings. Christie became that surrogate "niece" she wished she'd had. Maybe that's what had happened in Drew's case.

"Do you have time to run up to Slim's? Do you still have those wedding photos on your phone?" Christie asked.

"Yes and yes. Why?"

"I want to see if Slim recognizes any one of the people at the reception. I don't know if the aunt and uncle were there, but if Slim recognizes Charles, it's one more bit of proof that Drew is connected to the Donaldsons."

"But that doesn't prove anything other than a relationship."

"It puts at least one Donaldson in the same location where two deaths, twenty-five years apart, occurred. The sons may have also been there, and perhaps you caught one or more in your pictures."

"Okay. Let's go talk to Slim."

Slim had opened the gate by the time they arrived a few minutes later and was sitting in the faded Adirondack chair in front of his cottage, a beer in hand.

"Thanks for meeting with us, Slim," said Christie. "We have some photos from the wedding last weekend that we'd like to have you look at."

Anita handed him her cell phone and showed him how to scroll through the two dozen or so photos.

"What do you expect me to find in them?"

"I'm not sure there will be anything, but tell us if you recognize any of the people at the reception, please."

Slim looked at each photo carefully, squinting and shaking his head after most of them. After several minutes, he sat up straight, rubbed his neck, and pointed to the screen. "That guy in the back, sitting with the woman wearing a blue dress. That's Charles Donaldson. I'd swear to it."

"You're sure?" Christie asked. "What about the woman?"

"That's Norma Lindemann, his sister. My boss."

# CHAPTER THIRTY-FOUR

"Norma Lindemann? The woman who owns Langley Manor now?" Christie asked, her heart thumping in her chest.

"Yes. Definitely." He returned the phone. "What was she doing at this wedding? Norma doesn't usually show up at the events here. She has me do all the prep work and doesn't come until the next day to clean up."

"Did you recognize anyone else, like any of the sons?"

"I looked pretty good at those faces, but those teenage boys would be in their forties by now and would look a lot different. If any of them were there, I couldn't tell you for sure. And I didn't live here then, so I didn't know them very well at all."

"Thanks, Slim. I'm going to share this information with the detective. He might want to talk with you about the photos, if that's okay with you."

Slim sat back, shaking his head. "That's pretty strange, the Donaldsons coming back here after all these years. You're thinking it has something to do with the second girl dying, don't you?"

"Yeah, I do. There are too many coincidences here. They've got to be connected somehow."

"You'll let me know, won't you, Ms. O'Mara?"

"Of course. I'll tell you before I tell anyone else."

IT WAS ALREADY late afternoon on a Saturday, but Christie didn't want to wait until Monday to talk to McAvoy. He agreed to swing by her house to look at the photos. She'd asked Anita to forward all of them to her so she could look at them on her computer's bigger screen. Jason wanted to come by as well when she told him what she'd learned.

The three of them huddled over Christie's laptop on the dining room table. Christie pointed out the man Slim had identified as Charles Donaldson and his sister, Norma Lindemann.

"So you hadn't met Mrs. Lindemann prior to the wedding?" McAvoy asked.

"No. All the communication was over the phone and email," replied Christie. "Slim took care of opening the gate and all that. Like he told me, she doesn't come down from Olympia unless she has to."

McAvoy sat back in his chair. "And you're sure Charles Donaldson is the uncle that Mrs. Simpson referred to?"

"No, but his being at this wedding certainly suggests that there's some kind of relationship between the Simpsons and the Donaldsons. It'll be up to you to verify it and find out what the actual relationship is."

"I have the wedding guest list at the station," said McAvoy. "I can have Officer Newell cross-check it for names and see if there are any other Donaldsons on the list. Do you know the sons' names, by any chance?"

"Just a minute and I'll get my notes," said Christie. She

returned a moment later with her notebook. "The boys are now men, of course. Alex was the oldest, and he would be about forty-three now. He lives in Poulsbo and is a math teacher. Next was Daniel, sixteen then, forty-one now. He's a financial consultant in Tacoma. The youngest was Samuel at fourteen. He went into the army, spent twenty years in the service, and is now a military recruiter in Fresno."

"You got that from Ben?" McAvoy looked between Christie and Jason.

Jason answered, "Yes. He also checked Pastor Smith's background but couldn't find anything on him as far back as twenty-five years ago, when this all happened."

"I'll have Newell track these men down and see what he can learn. I'll also have him talk to some more guests to confirm that Charles was at the reception. I'd like to have more eyewitnesses to that effect. Good work, Christie."

"And Ben," Christie added, nodding to Jason. "You might have Newell ask which of them was friends with Jeremy, and what his last name was. Surely one of them would know, or perhaps you can get that from Mr. or Mrs. Donaldson."

"We'll start on it today. I'd like to solve this murder. Lauren deserves that." McAvoy stood and tipped his hat. "I can find my way to the door," he said with a wink.

"What do you want to do now, Christie?" Jason asked once they were alone.

"I'm still curious about why Lauren was at that wedding. She seems to be the link between the two murders. I think she learned something that she wanted to follow up on. But what motivation did she have to go to a former boyfriend's wedding? That is, if he indeed was a boyfriend—or fiancé."

"We could follow the trail of that fifty thousand dollars and see whose account it went into."

"That's a good idea," said Christie. "Lauren would be my

first bet. I could call Mrs. Elliott and see if she has access to Lauren's bank records."

"No. It would be better to ask McAvoy to get the information through his legal channels."

Christie nodded, chagrinned. "Even if Lauren was the recipient, that doesn't explain why she went to the wedding and why she was on the widow's walk. If I were the jilted fiancée, I'd be sitting right where Drew could see me as he faced the guests. Like on the end of a pew. And if I'd gotten fifty thousand bucks to back off, I'd be more than happy to do just that." She shook her blonde curls. "What was she doing there?"

"Tell you what. I'll call McAvoy and get him started on this money issue while you think. I'll offer Ben's services if he can't get through to the bank directly."

"Good idea. Lauren's account was probably at the bank in Elida where she was working, unless she hadn't moved her account yet from Chehalis. I'll call Mrs. Elliott and find out which bank it was."

"Good idea."

Christie took a big breath and called Lauren's mother.

"Mrs. Elliott? This is Christie O'Mara again. I'm so sorry to bother you, but I'd like to follow up on an idea that might be related to Lauren's dying."

"I'll do anything to help you. What do you need to know?"

"Where did Lauren have her bank account? Is it where she started working recently?"

"No, not there. It's at the State Bank in Chehalis. That's where she was going to college, and it was more convenient for her."

"Thank you. That's very helpful."

"I could look for her bank statements, if you like. I'm sure they're in her room somewhere."

"Sure. I'll wait while you look. Thanks."

Christie idly doodled on the open page of her notepad while listening to the dog barking in the background, then a door closing, then virtual silence for the next few minutes.

"Hello? Are you still there?"

"Yes, Mrs. Elliott. Did you find anything?"

"Not the bank statements. She must have already put them through the shredder in her room. But I found something else."

"What?"

"It's her mother's diary, or maybe you call it a journal. Anyway, I didn't know she'd found it."

# CHAPTER THIRTY-FIVE

Jason pulled up in front of the Elliotts' home. Christie jumped out of the car and ran up the short sidewalk to the door. She heard the dog barking even before she rang the bell.

Mrs. Elliott met her at the door a few seconds later and handed her the journal. "I couldn't ever bring myself to read it. I don't know when Lauren found it, but I hope it's helpful to you."

Christie took the journal using a tissue and slipped it into a Ziplock bag she'd grabbed as she and Jason left her house. "Thank you. Maybe there is a clue that will explain Lauren's death in here. I'll get it to the detective right away. I'll stay in touch." She waved goodbye and hurried back to the car.

She opened the journal with great anticipation, being careful to use a tissue to avoid adding her own fingerprints. She started turning pages while Jason drove back to White Castle. "The first date in here is January 1, 1999. It looks like she didn't write every day, more like once a week."

Christie read through several months of entries before

finding something worth sharing with Jason. "I gather that she was a teacher at one of the schools in the Olympia area, although she doesn't specify which one. Her mom might know. Anyway, she mentions that someone at the school has started to pay attention to her."

"Does she give a name?"

"Not yet. I'll keep reading. Most of what she writes about is what she did on the weekends, or something special that one of her students did, like a major achievement."

Jason turned on the radio for company because Christie was unusually quiet.

"Here's an interesting comment. Cynthia writes, 'Skip asked me if I was free for dinner tomorrow night. I'm not sure what to wear.' "

"No name yet?" Jason interjected.

"No, but I'm not done yet." Christie flashed a little grin to Jason. "This is several weeks later where she writes, 'Skip has been leaving messages in my mailbox at school. I think I'm flattered but I know he's married. Mother would definitely not approve but I like him.'"

"What date are you up to?"

"February 2001. She's been journaling less often, but this one is very interesting: 'Skip proposed a weekend getaway to the beach. He says he has a condo at Ocean Shores and we would have it all to ourselves. I've stopped asking him about his wife. He says they're more or less separated. I'd rather he were divorced but that's not really my business. I haven't said I'd go yet, but I probably will. He treats me really well.' "

"So they're having an affair, but they haven't consummated it yet?" Jason asked.

"That's what I gather, but things look like they're about to change, I think. Next entry isn't until April 9, 2001. She writes, 'Enjoyed three days at the condo at the end of spring break. He says he loves me and that he plans to get divorced. I want to believe him but he's also at least twenty years older than I am, so what am I doing? I need to end this relationship before it ends badly.' I would guess the affair has now been consummated," said Christie. "It's hard to avoid sex when you're in the same room with a guy you like for three days."

"No comment," said Jason. "Keep reading."

"Okay. Next comments are more of the same. He leaves her love notes in her cubby in the teachers' lounge. More flowers. Every Saturday, she says. Uh-oh... She did a pregnancy test and it's positive. She writes, 'He swore he'd had a vasectomy, so how is he going to explain this? I haven't been with anyone else in months and months! He'll have to get that divorce now for sure.' "

"Yep, consummation has taken place," Jason said in sportscaster style.

"Jason! This is serious." Christie reached over and slugged him in the arm. "The next note is a few days later. 'Skip says his wife has cancer and he can't leave her right now. When I told him about the pregnancy test, he said new responsibilities could ruin him... he made me promise never to tell. But who would I tell? He even asked if it was possible for me to get an abortion. The jerk!'" Christie felt angry on Cynthia's behalf.

"I agree that he was a jerk," said Jason, sensing Christie's mood.

She flashed him a smile and resumed reading. "She's back to writing every week again, mostly about pregnancy symptoms, and a few comments about having to tell her mother about it. 'I can't tell her who the father is. I'm too ashamed that I let myself get involved with a married man.' She tells her mom that it was a guy she was dating for a while but that he isn't marriage material, her teacher buddies throw a baby shower, and so on." Christie leaned back in the passenger seat.

"The journal ends in January 2002. She has a baby girl, names her Lauren. She writes, 'I won't give him the pleasure of having his name on the birth certificate. I haven't seen him in at least four months and never want to see him again.' That's it."

"She never identifies this guy by a name except as 'Skip'?" Jason asked.

"Correct. Although it seems like he'd have to be a teacher because of access to the teachers' lounge. But I suppose it could be someone in administration as well." Christie groaned. "It might be hard to find out which teacher with a nickname of 'Skip' was teaching in one of the Olympia elementary or middle schools in 2001."

"I'll bet Ben would have a list of names in a few minutes, but knowing who went by 'Skip' will be harder, especially if that wasn't a real nickname. He could have been using a fake name to hide his affair. I can call him when we get back to White Castle."

"Or it's a name that Cynthia used in her journal for the same reason—to hide his real identity. You know, I wouldn't be surprised to learn that Lauren did that same research already, and it's probably on her laptop that I gave to McAvoy last Sunday," said Christie. "He should be able to use it to see what she researched and how it fits with this."

Christie had already started a call to McAvoy without waiting for Jason to respond. "Hey, McAvoy. Christie here. I've been reading Lauren's mother's diary, and I believe she searched for her biological father with the information she found in it. If Lauren found the answer from her internet search already, it might only be clear when compared to the journal. It would save a lot of time for you to compare what's in the journal to her laptop research."

"That sounds reasonable. I hate to admit that it's already been a week since she died and we haven't made much progress. I don't have anyone available on the weekend who can do that." He paused. "Listen. The laptop isn't considered evidence at this stage, so would you mind doing that comparison? I'm out in the field today. Meet me at the station. That's where the laptop is."

"Perfect. We can be there in ten minutes."

McAvoy was waiting in his patrol car when Jason and Christie pulled up.

"What kind of information did she find?"

"Lauren's father's nickname was Skip, and he was working at one of the schools in Olympia," said Christie. "It isn't clear whether or not he was a teacher or an administrator, but maybe the personnel records would have that detail."

"Sure. The schools were probably all digitalized by that time," said the detective.

Christie nodded. "We know she was born in 2002, and the schools were definitely using the internet by then. May I have permission to search her history?"

McAvoy nodded. "Lauren was only twenty-three." He shook his head, his face grim. "Go ahead—and keep me posted."

# CHAPTER THIRTY-SIX

Christie and Jason sat at her dining table with the laptop open for business. The Canadian bacon-and-pineapple pizza that Jason had picked up at Vernie's on the way from the police station to her house was half-eaten.

"I'm getting a headache from this," said Christie. "Where do you think she kept notes on what she found out?"

"Try looking in her document files. She may have set up a running list that she could add to as she found new information. That's what I do when I'm working on a case at work," said Jason.

"Great idea. Let's hope she gave it a logical name," she added with a groan. A moment later, she said, "Lauren seems to think like I do. The file is named *The mysterious Skip*. Not very original but clever. Now, let's see what's in it."

Several minutes passed as Christie scrolled and jotted down notes. "She made phone calls to all the elementary and middle schools in Olympia and Lacey. Looks like she ran into some confidentiality issues along the way and couldn't get all the names." She sat back in the chair and stretched her back. "Sitting like this reminds me of when I was working for the furniture company. I spent a lot of time with a backache, staring at numbers on a computer. I'm glad I'm not doing that anymore."

"Do you truly like owning your own business? In a way, it's a lot more work," said Jason.

"Yeah, I suppose I put in more than the so-called forty-hour work week, but it's much more satisfying to see my customers smile, and I get to use the creative side of my brain. Financially, I'm doing okay. At least I haven't had to ask Mom and Dad for a loan yet." She laughed. "Back to the mysterious man who's even more mysterious now that he seems to have a confidential file."

"I haven't called Ben yet. If you forward everything to me that she has in that file, I'll have him dig deeper into the web."

"He can get into confidential files?" Christie exclaimed. "Then how can they be called confidential?"

"You'd be surprised at how easy it is to access information like that when you know where and how to look. I'll give him a call in a few minutes, and we can tackle something else."

"Okay, Jason. I'm forwarding the file to you now."

"And didn't you mention something about newspaper archives related to Lauren's mother's car accident?"

"Yes. Thanks for reminding me. I took pictures of the articles at Mrs. Elliott's house. She had the originals and let me see them." Christie quickly pulled up the photos she'd taken on her cell and sent them to her printer while Jason called Ben.

Jason and Christie each took one of the three pages to read.

"This news item is from the night of the accident," said Christie. "It happened on Highway 12 near Randle on April 1,

2004. It was raining and the roads were slick. She was alone in the car. She apparently lost control of the late-model SUV and slid into a power pole. Killed instantly." Christie looked up with a quizzical look on her face. "She didn't have Lauren with her, so who was taking care of her? Had she been drinking? Was there someone else in the car who left the scene?"

"Always the suspicious one, aren't you?" Jason said as he finished reading his page. "This follow-up article says that Cynthia Elliott was a single mother and was on her way to a three-day retreat in Central Washington during spring break. Her daughter, Lauren, was staying with Cynthia's mother in Lacey. No other next-of-kin were named here."

Christie picked up the third page. "This one is about the funeral service planned at the Eastside Baptist Church in Olympia." She sighed. "It's so sad that she died alone, and that she left a tiny daughter behind."

"You know yourself that the road conditions on that highway can be really treacherous in early spring. There's often a late snowfall in April. And if it was anywhere close to freezing, black ice is a real possibility. She wouldn't have to be driving very fast to get in trouble very quickly if that were the case."

"Granted." She was lost in thought for a moment. "I wonder if the authorities checked for mechanical issues at the time. What if it wasn't an accident?"

"If they didn't check at the time, it'll be impossible to assess mechanical issues at this date. We'll just have to assume facts in evidence and that the car was mechanically sound."

"But what if it wasn't?"

"There's no way to check, Christie. Let it go."

"Humph. I wonder if Mrs. Elliott recalls anything else about the accident or about Cynthia's activities at the time. I wish she'd continued her journal, but she probably was writing in her daughter's baby book instead."

Christie jumped when her phone rang in her pocket.

"Hey. It's Stephanie. You remember, the maid of honor."

"Hi, Stephanie. What did you find out?"

"I talked to Lindy, and she said it was definitely a male voice and a female voice that she heard that day we were dressing for the wedding. They were pretty loud, but she didn't recognize either one. She's sure they weren't in the hallway, but they could've been in that other room, I suppose, instead of up on the widow's walk, which we didn't know about anyway. We're both sure that it wasn't any of the people in the wedding party. We were all getting ready for pictures and nobody was missing from our group."

"Very good. Thanks," said Christie. "Did you by any chance learn anything more about the fifty thousand dollars?" She crossed her fingers.

"Maybe. We girls were talking about that a few days ago when we had drinks over at the Grotto. You know, that new bar on Main Street."

"I haven't been there yet, but yeah. What did you find out?"

"Lindy's mom works at the bank in town, and she took the Fifth when Lindy asked her if she knew anything. I think that means she *does* know something but can't talk about it because of all those confidentiality laws and all."

"Those laws are important, Stephanie," said Christie. "But that's useful information even without names. Anything else?"

"Um, I don't think so. We're going to have drinks with Drew and Tiffany tomorrow. Do you want to join us?"

"I don't think so, but thanks for the offer," said Christie. "And thank you for the call." She smiled as she pressed the red phone icon.

"What was Stephanie's useful information?" Jason asked. "You're grinning like that Cheshire Cat in Wonderland."

"McAvoy will want to interview Lindy's mom—Lindy was one of the bridesmaids—at the bank. She knows something about a fifty-thousand-dollar transaction where she works at a bank right here in White Castle."

# CHAPTER THIRTY-SEVEN

"I just thought of another way we could find out who the mysterious Skip was," said Christie.

"What idea have you come up with now?" Jason asked.

"Here's my thought: Mrs. Elliott might recall the name of the school where Cynthia was teaching. And maybe even a teacher friend's name. I'll bet a few of those teachers are still there, or at least in the district. We can try calling some of them and see if they'll give us the answer. They might not know who the father of Cynthia's daughter is, but they might remember someone, possibly a teacher, who went by the name 'Skip.' "

"Excellent idea, Miss Detective." Jason did a mock bow.

Christie had Mrs. Elliott on the phone within sixty seconds. "Hi, Mrs. Elliott. Christie O'Mara again. I have a question that I hope you can answer."

"I'll do my best. Is it about Lauren?"

"No. It's about your daughter Cynthia."

"Oh! What's your question?"

"Do you remember the name of the school where she was teaching?"

"Um. Let me think a moment. It's been such a long time since I've thought about that."

"Take your time. It's important."

"Let's see... It was Lake something. Like Lake Capitol Elementary. Maybe Lake Lacey. Just a minute. I'll ask Frank."

Christie listened to muffled sounds in the background. A television was on in addition to the conversation between the Elliotts.

"Frank said it was Crystal Lake Elementary. It was one of the newer ones at the time on the west side of town. Why do you need to know?"

"Do you remember any of her close friends' names? Or one of the other teachers at the school when she was teaching there?"

"I remember her talking about a friend named Natalie a lot. Natalie Abbott, I believe, but she might have a different name by now, if she got married. I'm not sure she was a teacher, though."

"That's very helpful."

"By the way, how was the service for Lauren? Wasn't that earlier today?"

"Yes, it was." She sniffled. "Pastor Smith did a beautiful eulogy even though he didn't really know Lauren very well. And her co-workers from the bank were there, and Jazmine and a few other college friends that I didn't know. It feels like I've buried two daughters now. Lauren was like my own daughter, you know, after raising her since she was two." More sniffling. "Well, I must say goodbye to the pastor. He came by after the reception to make sure Frank and I were okay by ourselves. I do hope you find the information you're looking for."

"Thank you, Mrs. Elliott."

Christie scowled as she closed the connection.

"Why is that look on your face? Bad news?"

"No, but I'm wondering about Pastor Smith again. He's at the Elliott home. Lauren's service was today, and Mrs. Elliott said it was very nice."

"That's good."

Christie shrugged in reluctant agreement and went on to share, "She said Cynthia taught at Crystal Lake Elementary. That should help Ben with his research. And she had a friend named Natalie Abbott, who may have taught there."

"I'll pull up my white pages app right now," said Jason. "Sometimes I get lucky with name searches."

"With my run of bad luck recently, Miss Abbott could be married by now, with three kids and a different last name," said Christie. "Every time I get close to pinning down a useable piece of information, I run into a dead end instead." She collapsed into the back of the sofa where she'd been sitting since ending her stint at the computer. "Maybe I'm not meant to figure out either of the mysteries."

Jason walked across the room and joined her, placing a comforting arm around her shoulders. "It's just a bump in the road. Every piece of data helps piece it all together. And I found a number for Natalie Abbott in Lacey. Do you want to call her?"

"Hi, is this Natalie Abbott? This is Christie O'Mara in White Castle."

"Yes, I'm Natalie. Where's White Castle? I've never heard of it."

"It's a small town about twenty miles southeast of Chehalis, on Highway 12 heading to Mt. Rainier."

"Okay... How can I help you, Ms. O'Mara?"

Christie took a breath and crossed her fingers. "I'm calling because you may be the Natalie who was friends with Cynthia Elliott about twenty years ago."

"Yes. Cynthia and I were pretty close back then, right up until she died. She had a little girl—Lauren, I think was her name," Natalie said with a lilt in her voice. "How is her daughter? She'd be a young adult by now."

"That's partially why I'm calling. Unfortunately, Lauren died a week ago, and I'm trying to retrace some research she'd done about her biological father. Do you know anything about that?"

"I'm so sorry about Lauren. Can you give Cynthia's mother, Lauren's grandmother, my sympathies? I know she took in her granddaughter after the accident."

"Of course. What about her father? What do you know?"

"Well, that mystery went to the grave with Cynthia. She would never tell me who the guy was—she always referred to him as Skip. I don't know what his real name was. Anyway, I knew he was married and supposedly getting a divorce, and was about twenty years older than Cynthia was."

"Do you know what happened with him? I mean, why the relationship ended?"

"The schmuck kept making excuses as to why he wasn't getting a divorce, and Cynthia told me she finally cut off all contact. I'm not sure she ever talked to him again, whoever he was."

"Understood. Is there a chance that you recall the names of the teachers where you and Cynthia taught?" Christie felt her hopes rise.

"Cynthia was the teacher, not me. I'm an attorney practicing family law in Olympia."

"Oh, I'm sorry. Mrs. Elliott thought you might have been a

fellow teacher at Crystal Lake Elementary." Christie heard a soft laugh on the other end of the phone.

"No, but if I had been one of the other teachers, I could probably answer the question. I tried and tried to get Cynthia to go after this Skip to get child support, at least, but she was too ashamed to do that."

"Would you by any chance know who any of her fellow teachers were at the time? I'm at a dead end otherwise."

"I might be able to help you with that. Let me make some phone calls, and I'll get back to you. Is that all right?"

"That would be great, Natalie. Thanks."

Christie's shoulders drooped as she ended the call. "I felt sure she'd be able to help, but she's an attorney, not a teacher."

Jason gave her a hug. "Ben's working on it too, remember."

Christie jumped when her phone rang. Thinking it might be Natalie calling her right back, she answered before the second ring.

"Hi. It's Jazmine. I just remembered something."

"What did you remember, Jazmine? Is it about the wedding?"

"No. This happened a few weeks before all that. Lauren had been doing all kinds of research online recently to find out who her father was. I guess she thought that knowing his name would give her some comfort, even though he was obviously some kind of scumbag."

"That was Lauren's mother's conclusion as well. But I understand her wanting to know. It's one of those pieces of information that many adopted children long for, as if it would help them deal with having been rejected by their biological parents. But back to Lauren. What did she tell you?"

"She started reading about DNA testing and how it can help people find other relatives. One of the ladies she worked with at the bank mentioned that she'd found a half-brother that way. So Lauren did the swab thing and got the results recently. She didn't tell me who it was, but she said she might have discovered who her father was and that she was going to try to contact him, but I wasn't supposed to tell anyone about it yet. So I didn't."

"Thanks, Jazmine. We have her laptop and should be able to find the results, unless she deleted them. Did she say anything else?"

"Not that I recall. I don't really understand why, but she was pretty excited to finally know who this person was. Now I wonder if she's dead because of it."

"We'll get right on it," said Christie. "Thanks for calling."

She and Jason huddled over the laptop while Jason searched through Lauren's many bookmarks. Thirty minutes later, they hadn't found anything that looked like DNA testing results.

"I'm afraid this is a job for Ben," said Jason.

"Drat!" said Christie. "Every time we get a bit of a clue, there's another roadblock."

# CHAPTER THIRTY-EIGHT

Christie held her head when she awakened Sunday morning. She and Jason had tried some fancy drinks at the Grotto along with a spicy chicken dish. She wondered if it was the spice, the alcohol-heavy drinks, staying up too late, or some combination thereof that caused the headache. She even found herself wondering if this was a migraine. Figuring she was too old to start having them now, she made a pot of extra strong coffee. By ten o'clock, after a mugful of full-strength caffeine, her headache had abated and she was ready to tackle her mystery anew, armed with the new information.

Stormy curled up in her lap while she read through her notes. Then she scrolled through Lauren's search history—again—hoping to find whatever had triggered Lauren's own fateful visit to Langley Manor. Ten minutes later, she found a reference to the Donaldson family. Lauren had discovered that they were the previous owners of the manor, but she didn't indicate any relevance of that information.

Christie tapped her fingers on the keyboard as she wondered what Lauren's thought process might have been. Why did she care about that bit of ownership enough to write it down? Was it related to Adam's interest in the ghosts that he thought were there? Or something else?

She pounded her fist on the padded arm of the sofa. She simply didn't know enough about Lauren to figure out what the young woman might have been thinking. But what was it? Was it the DNA results that they hadn't been able to find?

She sipped on a second mug of coffee while she waited for her headache to fully abate. She'd finally taken two ibuprofen when the coffee by itself hadn't worked. When she was a little girl, her grandfather O'Mara used to tell her that black coffee would put hair on her chest. For years, she added coffee creamer until she decided to risk getting hair on her chest. She was still waiting but no longer worried about it. She smiled at the thought of her dear grandfather.

Stormy lay on the sofa next to her, purring softly as she dreamed happy kitty dreams. She jumped and meowed in protest when Christie's cell phone rang.

She recognized Natalie Abbott's number and felt a thrill of anticipation.

"I have a possible name for you," Natalie said. "One of Cynthia's former teacher friends shared a list of all the teachers and staff from Crystal Lake for the school years that she taught there."

Christie felt her heart thumping, maybe from adrenalin or perhaps too much caffeine.

"Who is it?"

"There were six men who taught and one male vice principal who would have been older than Cynthia. She didn't know Cynthia well enough to guess which one she was seeing, but all but two of them were married. That narrows it down to five names."

"That's great information, Natalie," Christie replied. Her headache miraculously disappeared. "Would you have contact information as well?"

"She gave me some old numbers, which I'll text to you along with the names."

"Thank you. I'll let you know what happens."

"Please do. And don't forget to tell Mrs. Elliott that I'm so sorry about Cynthia and Lauren."

Christie held the phone to her chest and smiled. Maybe she was getting closer to the answer. She almost dropped the phone when it buzzed unexpectedly against her skin.

Jason's name lit up the screen.

Her heart still beating harder than usual, she answered on the first ring. "Hi, Jason. Do you have some new information?"

"Good morning, Christie. I sure do. I'm tempted to ask you to join me for lunch and make you wait for it."

"That would be cruel and unusual punishment, Mr. Princeton. And bribery too. Isn't it unethical for you attorney-types to do such a thing?"

Jason chuckled in her ear. "Only if we get caught. I'm serious about taking you to lunch, unless you're busy."

"I have some information too. If you want to share what you know, then I'll tell you what I know," Christie teased. "And we can still do lunch."

"You go first, Miss Detective."

"Okay. I just chatted with Cynthia's friend Natalie Abbott in Olympia. She gave me five names from Crystal Lake Elementary. I'll forward them to you as soon as I get the details that Natalie is texting to me."

"Great."

"One of them might be Lauren's father."

"Interesting, but being Lauren's biological father doesn't make him our murderer. And there are five names to investigate."

"But one of them might be the connection to both Debra Ellen twenty-five years ago and now maybe to Lauren."

# CHAPTER THIRTY-NINE

Lunch at The Grille was always a treat. The food was tasty, plentiful, and right-priced. They happened to hit the sweet spot of the day when the after-church crowd hadn't yet arrived and the early eaters had pretty much emptied out.

"What's your news, Jason?" Christie asked while perusing the menu. "Is it something that Ben uncovered?"

Jason smiled and nodded. "He made some discreet inquiries and found an interesting deposit of fifty thousand dollars into an account in Lauren's name at an Olympia bank."

"Mrs. Elliott said Lauren's bank account is in Chehalis."

"That may be true, but that's her current account. This was a custodial account connected to Cynthia Elliott's primary account."

"I don't understand. She died twenty years ago. Why would she still have an account?"

"It's a custodial account. Cynthia died without naming a beneficiary to her account. She was young and single and obviously wasn't thinking about dying anytime soon. But someone who was savvy in the financial world created an account for Lauren with a fifty-thousand-dollar deposit shortly after Cynthia died."

"So, it might not be a recent deposit that Tiffany mentioned when she was talking to Drew on the phone at all. You're saying it's from years—actually, two decades—ago."

"So it would seem."

"Who? Did Ben figure out who opened the account?"

"He has the name of the attorney who did the work, but he hasn't traced the origin of the money yet."

"Can't you just contact the attorney's office and find out that way? Why wouldn't Cynthia's mother be contacted for something like that?

"Too many questions, Christie. It's in a shroud of privacy, and I don't have all the information yet."

"Is the money still in the account?"

"Yes, with twenty or so years of interest."

"Hm. So who gets the money now?"

"Typically, it would go to her next-of-kin, which is probably Cynthia's mother."

The table server took their orders: waffles with a side of bacon for Jason; two eggs over easy with bacon and hash browns for Christie.

"You'd think Mrs. Elliott would've known about this account and used it for Lauren all these years."

"That's a logical assumption," said Jason, "but it assumes she knew about it."

"I think it was Skip, feeling very guilty about the whole situation."

"Also a logical assumption, but we don't know that yet. Nor do we know Skip's real name."

"I could call Mrs. Elliott and see if she knew about that money."

"You could, but I say you wait until Ben has a name for us—the depositor's name, I mean. I know she wanted you to stay in touch, but you've been bugging her a lot this week."

Christie reluctantly agreed.

"Now you can tell me your news. That was the deal."

"Right. Well, now my information isn't as exciting as I thought it was. I was sure Charles Donaldson was guilty of two murders when Natalie, Cynthia's friend, gave me those names and his name was on the list. Maybe he's only guilty of one."

"Or none," cautioned Jason. "There's still the possibility that Drew snuck up to the widow's walk to meet Lauren, strangled her, and that she managed to crawl to the stairs and fall down and break her neck.'

"Or it could've been Adam, for that matter," replied Christie. "Someone had to unlock the padlock to get up there, unless those instructions about unlocking it in the text messages were enough for Lauren to do it herself. And the waiter described Adam perfectly, when I finally met him."

"I don't know what motive Slim would have for murdering Lauren, but I suppose he has to stay on the list."

"I don't think he did it. I saw him limping at the wedding. But I could ask Mrs. Lindemann about it, I guess, in case he was faking it."

"Good idea," said Jason as the server arrived with their steaming plates. "Here's our food. Let's eat."

Christie sat at her dining table with her notebook. She wanted to call Mrs. Elliott and ask her about the money Ben had discovered in the Olympia bank. She wasn't sure how she was going to open the discussion, with Lauren's death so recent. And she knew she should wait, like Jason said, until they got more information, but what would it hurt to find out now? Thankfully, her cell phone rang before she had another moment to consider how to start the conversation.

It was Jazmine again. “Christie? It’s Jazmine.”

“Yes, what’s on your mind, Jazmine?”

“Well, I’m not sure it’s anything, but Tiffany just called me and asked me a weird question.”

“What kind of weird question?”

“She wondered if the detective she talked with could really go back twenty-five years to try to solve an old murder. When I said I didn’t know, she started babbling about a murder that had occurred many years ago at the same place where she got married and how it could ruin everything.”

“I don’t understand. Did she explain further?”

“She’d told Drew what you said about the detective going back and investigating that old murder. He got really upset and said he needed to talk to his father about it. So he left the house, and she wasn’t sure where he went.”

“Wouldn’t he have gone to his father’s house? That seems logical to me.”

“Tiffany said she called her mother-in-law, who said Mr. Simpson had gone out somewhere to meet with Drew, but she didn’t know where.”

“Perhaps she should talk to the detective herself. McAvoy might be able to help her.”

“She doesn’t dare do that. Drew’s dad has a pretty bad temper, especially when he thinks he’s being crossed.”

“Gee, I don’t know what to tell you, Jazmine, but thanks for calling me. And if you talk to her again, you can tell her that there’s no time limit, as far as I know, in an unsolved murder case.”

Christie stared at the blank screen on her phone. *What is Drew worried about?*

# CHAPTER FORTY

Christie helped her mother finish making the salad and set the table for dinner. When she and Jason and her parents were finally seated, it occurred to her that it was a little like the command performance of dinner on Sundays on one of her favorite programs, *Blue Bloods.* She enjoyed watching the reruns as much as the first viewings of the episodes because she'd missed so many of them over the years.

Once the blessing of the meal was done, her mom, Maureen, asked Jason about a case that involved one of the hospital volunteers. He politely demurred as the case hadn't gone to trial yet. Her father, Tom, asked what Jason thought about the Mariners' chances in baseball this year. Then Maureen put Christie on the spot about the Langley Manor murder.

"All my friends think it was that boyfriend who's responsible," said Maureen. "What's a mother to do when her daughter's friends aren't the sort of people you want in your own home?"

Jason and Christie rolled their eyes at each other, then laughed.

"It's not funny, Christie O'Mara. I would die a thousand deaths if it were you getting killed like that Elliott girl."

"I know, Mom. I'm careful about my friends." She smiled at Jason.

He reached across the table and squeezed her hand.

"Of course you are," she acquiesced. "Now, how's that landscape design business of yours coming along?"

"It's going well. Anita has two new prospective clients who've asked for consultations this week. She's thinking we may have to contract out for some of the physical labor when people ask for retaining walls and that sort of thing."

"Great. Your father and I should carry a few of your business cards so we can hand them out if the opportunity arises."

"Wonderful, Mom. Should've thought of that before. Thanks."

Apple pie à la mode was the crown jewel of the meal.

"Great food, Mrs. O'Mara. I hope you taught Christie how to cook like this," Jason said.

Christie felt her face redden as she realized the implication of that statement. She shook her head. "Not my bailiwick. Besides, I was too busy with sports when I was in high school."

Christie's mother laughed. "Please call me Maureen, Jason. Or I'll have to call you Mr. Princeton."

The laughing was interrupted by Christie's phone ringing in her pocket.

"It's Pastor Smith. I wonder what he wants. Excuse me." She stepped into the living room and pressed the green icon.

"This is Pastor Smith. We need to talk."

"Yes, Pastor. What do you want to talk about?"

"Can I meet you somewhere? I don't want to do this over the phone."

"Sure. Tomorrow, I'll be—"

"We need to talk tonight," he interrupted.

"Oh. Um. How about my flower shop in White Castle? You know where that is."

"Yes, that would be a good place. I can be there in about forty minutes. Does that work?"

Christie glanced at her watch. It was already 6:30. "That would be fine."

All eyes were on her when she returned to the table. "He wants to talk about something. I agreed to meet him at the shop at 7:15."

"I'm going to go with you," said Jason. "In case you need back-up."

"He's a pastor, Jason. Of course I'll be okay with him."

"You said Stormy hissed at him. I trust her judgment more than yours."

"I was going to ask you to join me anyway," said Christie with a grin. "We can go grab a drink at The Grotto afterward."

Pastor Smith was at the shop promptly at 7:15. Christie unlocked the front door when she saw his Camry. "Come on in, Pastor. We can chat at my consultation desk."

Jason stood as they approached and offered his hand. "Hello. I'm Christie's friend, Jason Princeton. Pleased to meet you."

An awkward silence followed after the three of them sat down.

"What did you want to talk about, Pastor?" Christie asked. "Is it about Lauren?"

"Not directly. It's about Debra Ellen Lewis."

Christie felt the blood drain from her face. "Debra Ellen?

The young woman who died twenty-five years ago at Langley Manor?"

"Yes. That Debra Ellen." He breathed deeply. "I'm ashamed to admit that I was a coward that terrible night. I didn't know what to do when she was found dead, and I basically ran away."

"Are you the phantom boyfriend?" Christie asked with her heart thudding in her chest.

He shook his head. "No, nothing like that. She was very sweet and I liked her, but she was dating Alex, the oldest Donaldson boy. He was my good buddy, so we all hung out together at the house a lot." He half smiled, perhaps recalling a fond memory. "On the night she died, we had all—the Donaldsons, I mean, and me and Debra Ellen—been at their house when it was time to go to the football game. Debra Ellen didn't want to go, so Mr. Donaldson said he'd take her home and meet us at the game a little later."

Christie felt a cold shiver even though the shop's thermostat was set at seventy-two. Jason placed a protective arm around her shoulders.

"It was already the second quarter of the game when he finally showed up. He said he'd stopped for gas because he'd forgotten to fill up earlier in the day and was driving up to Tacoma the next day. I didn't think anything about it at the moment, but I later realized he must have killed her during that time interval."

Pastor Smith bowed his head. A few tears crept down his face. "When we all got back to the manor, Mrs. Donaldson found Debra Ellen and called the police. She told me there was no reason for me to stay around, so I left. I hadn't been back here since, until I started seeing those blogs that Adam Lawrence was posting about Langley Manor. It brought back those terrible memories."

"I thought the friend's name was Jeremy. Your name is James."

"That's another thing I'm not proud of, but I legally changed my name to try to disappear. My name was Jeremy James Smithson, or JJ as my buddies called me. I went into the army—that's when I changed my name. I reversed my first and middle names and dropped the 'son.' After some soul-searching, I studied to be a chaplain during my twenty years in the army. I continued my ministry once I got out. I've discovered, however, that it's hard to counsel others about their sins when you have a big one of your own that you haven't faced."

"Do you want to talk to Detective McAvoy about this?" Christie asked gently. "He has the old case files and would like to hear you tell him yourself about that night."

Jason asked, "Why are you coming forward now? Do you think it has something to do with Lauren Elliott?"

"I don't know how to connect the two deaths, but when I saw that picture of the wedding a few days ago at your shop and recognized Charles Donaldson, I relived that awful night. And I decided I had to come forward about it." He rubbed his hands together fitfully.

"Why did you call me instead of the detective?" Christie asked with a furrowed brow.

"Mrs. Lindemann told me you'd been talking to the caretaker at the manor. She assumed it was about Lauren, but I was pretty sure she didn't know that Slim was Debra Ellen's uncle. I talked to him myself and almost told him that day who I really was, but I didn't have the courage."

"Was that earlier this week?"

"Yes, Tuesday, as I recall. How did you know?"

"My friend Anita and I were looking for the hole in the fence, and we saw you driving away from the manor," said Christie. "You were in a silver Subaru."

"I didn't see you, but yes, that was me."

"Okay, but you were in a white Camry at the Elliotts' home on Sunday."

"I had to borrow a car from one of my friends because mine was in the shop."

"So that explains the difference. I was confused," said Christie.

"Yes," he said with a laugh. "I certainly can't afford two cars on my salary!"

Christie nodded. "That makes two mysteries solved, if Mr. Donaldson really killed Debra Ellen."

"I believe he did," said the pastor, "but I'm not sure how to prove it. Of course I'll help the detective any way I can."

"Detective McAvoy will be glad to listen. I have another question: how did you know that Slim was Debra Ellen's uncle? Had you met him before?"

"I found out from Alex some time ago. We've stayed in touch and, yes, he knows about the name change and all that. Anyway, as far as I know, he hasn't told the rest of the family what really happened to me. They believe that I simply moved on and never looked back." He put his hands together as if in prayer. "That's only half true, as it turns out. A person can move on, but with my conscience, I couldn't avoid looking back."

"Do you have any ideas about how or why Lauren was killed last weekend?" Jason asked. "There doesn't seem to be any direct connection between Lauren's family and Debra Ellen's family. As an attorney, I prefer to work with tangible evidence."

"Not that I can come up with. Theresa Elliott told me that you'd taken her daughter's diary—Cynthia's, that is. She refers to both Cynthia and Lauren as daughters, as I'm sure you can understand. Did you learn anything helpful from it?"

"Well, that's a puzzle," said Christie. "Cynthia wrote about having an affair with a married man who was quite a bit older, but she never named him. She called him Skip, but her friend Natalie Abbott, with whom I've also talked, said she never revealed anything more about him. She never mentioned his job but he apparently worked, perhaps as a teacher, at Crystal Lake Elementary in Olympia. He was almost certainly the father of her daughter, Lauren."

"Yes. Theresa—I mean, Mrs. Elliott—always wondered why Cynthia kept the name secret. It seems the man should be more ashamed than Cynthia was. But perhaps he thought he was above facing facts." Pastor Smith scoffed. "I thought I was too, until recently."

Jason said, "My private investigator is searching records at Crystal Lake Elementary for the mysterious Skip as we speak. Hopefully, we'll be able to cross reference names and find the person who fits the criteria."

"That's good. Now, shall we contact the detective? I'm ready to tell him everything I know."

# CHAPTER FORTY-ONE

Christie was at the shop a little earlier than usual the next morning, but so was Aunt Doris.

"Hi, Auntie," she called cheerfully as she lifted Stormy to her perch.

"You're pretty chipper this morning, young lady. Have you solved your murders? I mean, the detective's murders?"

"One of them, anyway—or at least, I think so." Christie shared the high points of the conversation with Pastor Smith.

Pastor Smith's revelation about the night at Langley Manor twenty-five years ago ran through Christie's mind like an endless loop while she snipped flower stems for the next order in line.

If the pastor was telling the truth, and she believed he was, then Mr. Donaldson was the most logical person to have murdered Debra Ellen. She'd forgotten to ask the reverend about the rumor of her being pregnant, but he may not have known anyway. If she'd been pregnant, and if it wasn't Charles Donaldson who was responsible, Christie theorized that it could have been one of this teenage sons. Would he have murdered her because of that?

The Donaldsons all had alibis for each other, except that the father's alibi was now tainted by Pastor Smith's story, which Christie accepted as very possible. He wouldn't have had to use the passageway through the maid's quarters. No one else was there to witness the event anyway. He could have simply driven away, as Slim had suggested the first time they talked.

Figuring out a logical connection to Lauren was a different matter. Although she'd found the news clipping about the Debra Ellen murder, it shouldn't have had a direct bearing on Lauren. Unless she'd learned something else in her research that wasn't in the file Christie had read.

"What else did Lauren find out?" she asked herself out loud and went to retrieve Lauren's laptop from her tote.

"What are you talking about?" Doris asked. "What about Lauren?"

"She's the second murder at Langley Manor," said Christie as she opened the laptop again to Lauren's notes. She scrolled through several pages of disconnected random comments, looking for something—anything—that could be the connection between Lauren and Debra Ellen.

"Aha! I think I've found it!" She closed the laptop, whipped off her work apron, and grabbed her coat. "I have to go to the police station and talk to McAvoy. I'll be back as soon as I can."

Charles and Sarah Donaldson arrived at the police station promptly at ten o'clock Monday morning. Detective McAvoy had interviewed Pastor Smith earlier and was ready to handcuff Charles, but he wanted to hear the man's version of the story first. He'd reread the transcript from the case file and refreshed his memory of the main players that fateful night.

Charles now sat in front of him in the interview room. McAvoy noticed a mild tremor in both of his hands. Nervousness, perhaps. Chief Conway, newly returned from his training week, observed through the two-way window. Sarah waited in another room with Joyce, the receptionist, keeping her company.

McAvoy cleared his throat. "Mr. Donaldson, thank you very much for traveling from Olympia this morning. How was the traffic?"

"Not bad coming south because we—my wife and I—were heading away from town. It's a crawl going north, however, for all those people going to work in the city. I'm grateful to be retired and not have to commute anymore." He coughed. "Allergies, my doctor says."

"That's good. Do you understand that you're here because a witness has identified you as the possible murderer of Debra Ellen Lewis twenty-five years ago at Langley Manor?"

Charles shook his head vehemently. "I couldn't have killed that young lady. I'd already gone to the football game. She was still alive when we all left. That's what I told the police then, and I stand by it now." He gulped water from the glass sitting on the table in front of him. "There couldn't have been a witness to see me because I didn't do it!"

McAvoy nodded and waited a minute before saying, "I've just learned from Jeremy Smithson, your elder son's friend, that you stayed behind when everyone else left for the game. He said that you offered to drive Debra Ellen home so she wouldn't have to walk in the dark. Is that correct?"

"Yes, I did offer to drive her, but she would have been with the whole family in the Suburban, not alone with me. We would have dropped her off on our way. She declined and said she would get home on her own."

"You're sure about that?"

"Absolutely. I've kicked myself a thousand times for not insisting that she come with us. She said she was going to go with her friends to the game and one of them was coming to pick her up. I reluctantly agreed because it was getting late, and I wanted to see the kickoff. It was a big game that night with our main rival."

McAvoy scanned the notes from the interview twenty-five years prior. "Which team was White Castle playing against that night?"

"Toledo High School—long-time rivals in our league. We were playing for district championship that night. It was a huge crowd."

"Are you sure about that?" McAvoy asked quietly. "In 1995, you said that White Castle was playing Stevenson High. Which is correct?"

Charles sputtered. "Oh, I may have gotten it wrong. Toledo was the next weekend, I guess." He shook his head with a thin smile. "Details sometimes elude me."

McAvoy's face didn't reveal anything he might have been thinking.

"Have you been in contact with Jeremy since that night?"

Charles scoffed. "He disappeared after the football game that night. I always wondered if he knew something more about her murder, but we never heard from him again. Even the police couldn't find him when they wanted to ask him some questions." He lowered his head and let loose a big sigh, then looked up. "How is it he's shown up now? How did you find him?"

"I can't tell you right now, Mr. Donaldson." McAvoy stood.

"I'm going to have Officer Newell stay with you while I interview your wife."

"She'll tell you the same thing, just like when it happened twenty-five years ago."

"That may be true, but I have to talk to her anyway. I'm sure you understand."

~

CHIEF CONWAY OPENED the door to the room next door when McAvoy knocked.

"What did you think, Chief? Do you buy his story?"

Conway clenched his teeth. "It pretty much matches what he said during the first interview. But that slip-up about the game makes me wonder if he has some memory loss going on. It might be nothing, however."

"I thought the same thing. I asked about the game specifically to test his memory for detail. It was a huge rivalry back in the day, I guess. I was surprised that he gave me an incorrect answer."

Conway nodded. "Unfortunately, I don't think it's enough to invalidate the rest of what he says. Go ahead and talk to his wife and see if you can crack that alibi of his." He half smiled as McAvoy left the room.

McAvoy rejoined Charles while Officer Newell escorted Sarah into the interview room and then left with Charles. McAvoy placed a glass of water on the table for her.

"Thank you, Mrs. Donaldson, for driving down from Olympia this morning. I'm sure this is hard for you, but there's been a new development in the young girl's death at Langley Manor in 1995."

Sarah scoffed. "New information? What could have possibly developed this many years later?"

"It was a surprise to us as well, but please walk me through the evening as you remember it."

She huffed before starting in on her version of the night that Debra Ellen died. Her rendition was a virtual copy of what her husband had said. And it matched the transcript that McAvoy had in the file.

When she ended her story, McAvoy asked her, "Do you remember Jeremy Smithson?"

Sarah fainted and slumped over in the chair.

# CHAPTER FORTY-TWO

Christie entered the police office where she found Joyce on the phone with 911, Officers McAvoy and Newell in the interview room with Sarah Donaldson on the floor, and Chief Conway standing in the doorway with the husband.

The EMTs arrived within another minute or two. While they were busy with Sarah, who had already come around, Christie grabbed McAvoy.

"I need to tell you something that I found in Lauren's research notes," she said excitedly. "I missed it the first time when I read through because there were several pages of comments that didn't seem relevant."

"Go on."

"Lauren noted that Adam had told her about some guy who had started interacting with his blog when he started writing about Langley Manor. Adam had been researching all the haunted buildings in town, and he was particularly intrigued by Langley Manor because it was considered to be haunted."

Christie pulled some printed sheets of paper from her pocket. "I had to print this out so I wouldn't goof it up. This is what Lauren wrote: 'This guy calls himself 'JJ' and says he knows how to get up to the widow's walk. Adam had heard about the widow's walk being locked and was trying to figure out a way to check it out, but the old building is all locked up with a big gate on the driveway and everything.'"

"How is this relevant, Christie?"

"I don't remember if I mentioned that there was a text or email—I forget which—on Lauren's phone that had to do with unlocking a padlock. It has to be the lock to the widow's walk."

"So you think this 'JJ' told Adam how to unlock the padlock so he could get up there?"

"Yes, and maybe so he and Lauren could go to that wedding and be unobserved."

McAvoy shook his head. "I follow you, sort of, but how does that end up with Lauren being murdered?"

"The only way that JJ could've known about the padlock was if he was connected to the Donaldsons, who padlocked the widow's walk in the first place. Or maybe from Mrs. Lindemann, who kept it locked to avoid a second accident, although we don't know how well Adam knew her. And Pastor Smith told me yesterday that his nickname was 'JJ' when he was young. He's got to be the same JJ that was communicating with Adam."

McAvoy took off his hat and rubbed his head. "I'm still confused about how this all ties together, Christie. Please enlighten me."

"Here's one scenario that makes sense to me: It's all based on the notes and research I found on Lauren's laptop. Somewhere along the way, she finds her mother's diary and learns about the affair with Skip. She's able to learn his name, Charles Donaldson, maybe the same way I did, and does more research. The DNA testing may have identified Drew Simpson as being related to Charles, and she strikes up a friendship. Maybe she stumbles on that news clipping at his house or in the archives about the death of Debra Ellen. Or maybe Adam shows it to her, since he'd be researching the reason this manor is haunted. Anyway, she makes the connection between the Charles Donaldson of twenty-five years ago and the Charles Donaldson with whom her mother had the affair."

"I don't know, Christie. That's a stretch. What would she do with that information?"

"If it were me, I would try to prove it. I might try to talk with Mr. Donaldson and see how he reacts to meeting the daughter he'd never met. Maybe she was considering blackmailing him with the threat of exposing him to his family about his affair with her mother."

McAvoy frowned. "But if she thought he'd murdered Debra Ellen, why would she risk that?"

Christie shrugged. "According to the news article she'd found, he'd been cleared, so she may not have worried about that. In fact, Jazmine called me two days ago, all excited because she remembered that Lauren had sent for one of those DNA tests. Lauren told Jazmine that she'd identified her father and was going to try to talk to him."

Officer Newell knocked and opened the door. "Mrs. Donaldson is ready to answer a few questions now."

"I'll call you later, and we can finish this conversation then, Christie." McAvoy hurried out of the room.

Sarah Donaldson sat with Officer Newell at her side, a glass of water on the table in front of her. Her color had returned to normal and she seemed composed.

McAvoy smiled kindly and said, "Let's try this again, shall we? Please tell me what you know about Jeremy Smithson."

"He seemed like a nice young man," she said with a faint smile. "He was best friends with my oldest boy, Alex, and was around the house a lot of the time. I always thought he would grow up to be a teacher, maybe, like Alex wanted to be."

"What about the night of the tragedy? Was he there then?"

"Let me think a minute. No, not right at first. He had to do something for his dad, he'd told Alex, and was going to meet us at the game."

"So he wasn't there when you all left?

"No, I don't think so. Well, maybe he came just as we left and followed us with his own car... Yes, that must be what happened. It was already well into the first quarter of the game when he joined us, though. Or at least when I first noticed him."

"You're sure about that? I have the notes from the interview done the night Debra Ellen died. At that time, you swore that you all left together."

"Well, we more or less did, just in two different cars. Isn't that the same thing?"

"What about your husband? Are you sure he left with you? Or did he offer to take Debra Ellen home and meet you later?"

"Debra Ellen wasn't at the house for dinner that night. I don't remember what she said she was going to be doing that evening, but we didn't see her at all that night till after the game when we found her crumpled body upstairs." Sarah burst into tears.

Newell handed her some tissues from the box on the table.

Composed again a few minutes later, Sarah said with a sniffle, "I've never forgiven myself for not checking that night to be sure that the door to the widow's walk was locked." She looked straight at McAvoy, then turned to look at Newell. "But I didn't have a reason to. It was just always locked. And I had no idea anyone would be coming to the house while we were away at the game."

LEAVING the Donaldsons together in the interview room, Conway, McAvoy, and Newell huddled over the table in the small conference room.

"We've got three different versions of what happened that evening before the football game," said McAvoy, sitting with his elbows on the table, leaning forward. "Who's telling the truth?"

"And how do we know whose story to believe? Or maybe none of them are telling the truth," Newell added.

"I'm less concerned about twenty-five years ago than I am about the murder that occurred on our beat nine days ago now," said Chief Conway. "Sure, maybe these murders are connected in some way, but who murdered Lauren Elliott? Was it Charles Donaldson? What's his motive? If he deposited fifty thousand dollars in Cynthia Elliott's account years ago like Princeton's private investigator said—which, by the way, we haven't proven yet—it may have been to try to assuage his guilt." He walked around the room. "But I refuse to believe he would kill his own daughter."

"Adam Lawrence is still in the picture, boss," said McAvoy. "I don't know of a plausible motive, but it could've been a true accident if he indeed was the person on the widow's walk with Lauren. He doesn't seem to have any motive, but perhaps they argued and they struggled and she fell, resulting in an accidental death. "

"But what about the strangulation that the coroner said

occurred first? I think it takes some motive to do that," Conway said.

"That waiter, Oliver something, had opportunity," offered Newell. "He could've strangled Lauren, then run down the stairs in time to appear innocent and make up a story about seeing another guy leaving the reception quickly."

"What about Drew Simpson?" asked Conway. "Is he in the clear?"

McAvoy replied, "It seems so, but he could've slipped up the stairs and strangled her, then left her to fall down the stairs while she was alone and he was enjoying his reception."

"Again," Conway noted, "she was already dead by strangulation, so that doesn't wash. And wouldn't he have been noticed as missing from the reception?"

He stood in front of the door, hands on his hips. "So we have no physical proof that we can use to charge any of these men. By the way, I'll send those two water glasses to forensics for DNA testing. Anyway, their opportunities are iffy. And no clear motive either. Is that what you're saying?"

"There is one other idea that I'd like to follow up on," said McAvoy. "Christie O'Mara came by while we were busy with Mrs. Donaldson and said she may have found the bit of information that could solve both murders."

# CHAPTER FORTY-THREE

Christie glanced at the door when the chimes rang to signal a customer. Seeing that it was the detective, she took off her apron and met him at the sales desk.

"How did the interviews go? Is Mrs. Donaldson going to be okay?"

"She's fine. The EMTs checked her out, but it was just a fainting spell. The interviews were another story."

"How so? Didn't Pastor Smith's confession, if you can call it that, help?"

McAvoy half smiled. "He certainly had me believing his version of the story, but it may be just that—a story. Both of the Donaldsons had a different memory of the night. And Chief Conway reminded us that what matters more right now is solving Lauren's murder."

"That's true, of course, but what was the difference in the answers that the Donaldsons gave? If you can tell me, that is."

"The wife said that Debra Ellen wasn't even there when

they left for the game. The husband said he offered to drop Debra Ellen off on the way to the game, which means he remembers her being there, and that they were driving in the Suburban. He claims she declined and said she'd go with her friends who were picking her up."

Christie frowned. "Do you believe their stories from the first interview? Or do you believe what they're saying now?"

"Well, the husband named the wrong team as White Castle's opponent that night, but he seemed to have everything else correct. And the wife now said that Debra Ellen hadn't been at the house when the family left for the game. That doesn't fit with her story twenty-five years ago."

Stormy jumped down from her perch to get some kitty love from McAvoy.

"But that wouldn't have any bearing on Lauren's murder, would it?" Christie searched McAvoy's eyes for his answer. "Here's a scenario that keeps bubbling up in my brain. What if Mrs. Donaldson is the one who is telling the truth, or most of it? If the family went to the game together and Debra Ellen was left at the house, someone—perhaps her friend who was picking her up—killed her or strangled her and left her for dead. I mean, that was pretty much the conclusion the police came to twenty-five years ago, since everyone had an alibi, with all of them at the game together. One of the sons—like Alex, perhaps, because he was the one she was seeing—might know who that could've been."

"That version suggests that a male was picking her up," said McAvoy. "That doesn't seem likely if she was dating Alex."

"Maybe, but what if it was Jeremy, now Pastor Smith, who was supposed to pick her up and take her to the game? If Mrs. Donaldson now says Jeremy wasn't even with them that night, maybe Debra Ellen was waiting for him to show up to take her.

He's a family friend as well as Alex's friend. Maybe he tried to get too friendly with Debra Ellen and she fought him, and he killed her accidentally in a moment of passion."

McAvoy nodded. "That could be the answer. But Pastor Smith says now that Mr. Donaldson was the one left behind. The wife's story is more believable to me... that the family left together. Besides, why wouldn't Debra Ellen just go with the Donaldsons and let Jeremy follow later? Like you said, she was dating Alex."

"Either way, someone is lying. Maybe they're all lying. Even so, I think one of them knows what really happened at the wedding last week when Lauren died."

McAvoy tapped a finger on the top of the counter, his lips in a terse line.

Christie continued, "I think you should talk with Adam again. Lay out what you've learned and see if he can fill in any details. He was friends with Lauren, knows Pastor Smith and may have even met him, and he has connections with Jazmine as well as Lauren's grandparents. Plus, you might interview Alex, see what his version of the Debra Ellen story is."

She waited for a response but when McAvoy said nothing, she added, "I don't think Adam killed Lauren, and I think you agree with me. If you assure him he's not a suspect at this time, he may tell you more than he did last time."

McAvoy cocked his head. "There's nothing to lose with a second interview. I'll call him in. And Alex Donaldson too."

"One more thing that I haven't figured out. When I talked with Tiffany last week—"

"You talked with Tiffany? Unofficially, I hope," said McAvoy, shaking his head.

"Of course, unofficially. I delivered some flowers and we just chatted. I kinda mentioned that you were looking at the earlier death at Langley Manor." Christie shrugged. "A day or two later, Jazmine called me and told me that Tiffany was really worried about Drew. She'd told him what I'd said about a twenty-five-year-old case, and he got all upset and said he had to talk to his father. He left the house and had been gone several hours by that time. Why would my mention of an old case send Drew rushing off to see his father?"

McAvoy didn't answer. He put his hat on his head as he turned to leave. "I'll call Adam and get him in for a second interview."

CHRISTIE CHECKED THE TIME AGAIN. Three o'clock. A mere ten minutes had ticked by since McAvoy's departure. She wondered if he was angry with her because she'd talked with Tiffany. She resisted the temptation to call him to apologize, thinking it might make things worse instead of better.

She sat at her desk and finished the order for flowers and greenery to be delivered later in the week. A few minutes later, her phone buzzed. She whipped it out, certain it would be the detective. Her spirits fell to the floor when she looked at the screen.

"Hi, Anita," she said more cheerfully than she felt. "How did your day go today?"

"Grr. I hate this time of year, when the weather is so nice and the school year is almost ended and the students stare out the window when they should be paying attention to me."

Christie laughed. "My grades always dipped in spring quarter when I was in college. I was just like your students and could hardly wait for the end. Except for finals, of course. So, what's on your mind?"

"I got a call today for a landscape consultation. It's a home out near the country club. It might not pan out, but I thought we could go out together after you close your store. If you're free, that is."

"I'd love to join you. Are you driving?"

"I've got my landscape kit in the back of my SUV so, yeah. I'll pick you up at your house about 5:30."

Christie joined her aunt at the flower table.

Aunt Doris peered at her over her rimless half-glasses. "What's wrong? You've been moping around here ever since you got back from the police station. Did Detective McAvoy yell at you or something?"

"No, nothing like that." She smiled reassuringly at her sweet aunt. "He told me he was going to interview Adam Lawrence again, and I've been hoping to get a call any minute about it."

"You know he'll call once he's done. He has to contact him first, you know. What else is on your mind?"

Christie shared what she knew of the morning interviews with the Donaldsons and Pastor Smith, now revealed to have been Jeremy Smithson.

"Lauren died because of something that she found out about someone or something to do with Langley Manor." She stood stock still and stared off into the distance. "I just thought of something that Jazmine told me about someone paying fifty thousand dollars to another someone. Maybe it's not the same money that Jason's PI discovered sitting in Lauren's mother's account from twenty years ago."

"What are you thinking, Christie?"

"Hush money or blackmail, perhaps? Could Lauren have threatened Mr. Donaldson that she would reveal his secret affair with her real mother?" Christie slapped her hand on the table. "That would fit with what Tiffany said about the fifty thousand dollars and could explain why Lauren was at the wedding. She might have been planning to meet with Mr. Donaldson and get the money from him. And she didn't want her grandmother, Mrs. Elliott, to know, so she made up the story about going to a wedding at the other church."

## CHAPTER
# FORTY-FOUR

McAvoy finally called at 4:30. Aunt Doris had already left for the day after finishing the delivery orders that Heather, Christie's part-time assistant, had loaded into the van a few minutes before. Christie was eager to close up shop and get home so she could go with Anita on the landscape design consult.

"Hey, Christie. McAvoy here. I've left a message for Adam to call me when he's done with whatever he's doing, so I don't know anything new there. Officer Newell is contacting Alex Donaldson, thinking he may be able to tell us what really happened on the way to the football game that night."

"That's a great idea! Why didn't I think of it?" Christie teased.

"You kind of did suggest it—and not so subtly, I might add. I hope he doesn't tell me a fourth version of that night's events. Now, I'd like to hear more about that phone call from Lauren's friend about DNA testing."

"Jazmine didn't have specific information, like a name, but she said Lauren was pretty sure she'd identified her biological father and was going to try to contact him. I checked her laptop and couldn't find the results there, but I might not have looked in the right place. Or she didn't save them. Or something. Anyway, Jason's PI guy should be able to track it down much more easily."

"Agreed. I'll talk to Jason myself. Have you learned anything else? Unofficially, of course."

"Sort of. When I was looking for that DNA bit, I reviewed Lauren's notes—the ones she kept in a general file. She noted that Pastor Smith had told Adam that he knew how to get up to the widow's walk. It seems that would confirm that he was familiar with the house and is consistent with his story that he's the Jeremy who disappeared. Until now, that is."

"I'm pretty confident that Pastor Smith is indeed Jeremy Smithson," said McAvoy. "But I'm not sure I believe his version of what happened that night. It still doesn't solve Lauren's murder, and that's what we need to focus on."

"I know. Do you think it's possible that the fifty thousand dollars Tiffany talked about with Drew is connected to Lauren's murderer and not related to that old trustee account? That's a lot of money, but it wouldn't affect Tiffany unless it was a current situation, and Jazmine said she reacted pretty strongly to that news.

"I can picture Lauren being very angry when she learned who her father was, even if we don't know for sure who it is, and threatening blackmail or something of that nature. And maybe her father *is* Charles Donaldson, and since the Donaldsons are related to the Simpsons and—"

"We're working on all that," McAvoy interrupted her

"Okay. Did Jason mention that Stephanie, the young lady who was Tiffany's maid of honor, called me and said her friend Lindy asked her mom about a fifty thousand dollar transaction at her bank?"

"Is this a second fifty thousand?" McAvoy asked.

"Yes, or at least I think so. Lindy's mother works at the bank in town and said she couldn't talk about it when Lindy asked her if it was true."

"If *what* was true, Christie? I'm not following your logic—or lack of it—at the moment."

"Well, maybe you'll have to talk to Drew about it, because that's who Tiffany was talking to on the phone when she said something about fifty thousand dollars at her bachelorette party."

"It may be a wild goose chase, but I'll have Newell follow up on that," said McAvoy resignedly.

"And don't forget to talk to Jason."

McAvoy ended the call without saying anything in response.

Christie stared at the screen for a moment, then shrugged and pocketed her phone while collecting Stormy and a few items she wanted to take home. She mentally ran through her check list for closing the shop and stepped out the back door.

She felt a moment of panic when she saw a male figure leaning against her car and considered going back into the shop, but she'd already set the alarm. Then she recognized him.

"Hi, Drew. How can I help you?" She reached into her pocket and pressed the key fob to unlock her car. She reached out to open the back door when Drew grabbed her arm. Her heart raced as she considered her options. She quickly glanced up and down the alley but didn't see a single soul. Yelling for help seemed futile.

"I need my arm to put my kitty in the car, if you don't mind."

Drew released her but stood directly behind her, effectively blocking her from being able to move away from the car, or to the driver's seat.

"You need to stop asking questions about Lauren," he said when she turned around. He was right in her face.

"Why does it bother you if I ask questions? Detective McAvoy is okay with it."

"You're stirring up old stuff that doesn't involve you."

Christie tried to ease sideways toward the back of her car, but Drew stayed within inches of her. She could smell some kind of alcohol on his breath, and it wasn't a nice smell. She wrinkled her nose. "Have you been drinking? Is that why you're acting like this?"

Drew grabbed her arm again. "Stop asking questions. Stay away from my family."

"Do you mean your wife and parents? Or are you talking about more distant relatives, like Uncle Charles and Aunt Sarah?"

Drew released his grip on her arm. His jaw dropped open. "They're innocent. They've always been innocent."

"So I'm assuming you know about the murder at Langley Manor in 1995. A young girl died in almost exactly the same way as what happened to your friend Lauren." Christie frantically tried to remember the lessons from her class on self-defense about getting away when cornered, but they hadn't taught anything about what do to when holding a kitty at the same time.

Drew shrugged. "It was an accident then. It's an accident now. End of story."

"Detective McAvoy isn't so sure. He's the one you have to convince. Now, I need to go home before my friend reports me missing. And I need to feed my cat. She gets very angry when dinner is late." As if on cue, Stormy let out a loud meow that surprised even Christie. "See?"

Drew stepped back. “Stay out of this. I’m sorry about Lauren. I really am, but there’s nothing you can do to fix it.”

“Fix what?”

“Forget it.” Drew pulled his jacket more tightly around his neck in the breeze that had kicked up from the river in the late afternoon and turned to walk down the alley. Christie stood still, like a robot, and watched as he hopped into a newer BMW coupe. She asked herself how he could afford the monthly payments on something like that.

# CHAPTER FORTY-FIVE

"What do you mean Drew Simpson came by the shop?" Anita asked as they drove to the prospective client's home. "Did he want to buy flowers?"

"Not in the alley, he didn't," said Christie. "He was trying to intimidate me into dropping the investigation into Lauren's death."

"I presume you told him it was Detective McAvoy in charge, not you."

"Of course. Anyway, no harm done. He walked away and I'll tell McAvoy a little later, after this consult." Christie shrugged. "So, where are we going today? What kind of project are we looking at?"

"From what the client told me, it's an older home on a one-acre lot near the country club. It was built in 1945 when the golf course was in its infancy and belonged to one of the owners of the paper mill up the river."

"And he probably liked to play golf after work and wanted to live as close as he could to the only golf course within twenty miles," said Christie, with a snarky voice.

"I don't know about that because he's been gone a long time, but the current owners do play golf, or at least the husband does. Mrs. Simpson said..."

"Did you say Mrs. Simpson?"

"Yes, Mrs. Simpson."

"As in Tiffany Simpson?"

"No, as in Colleen Simpson." Anita turned to glance at Christie. "Do you suppose it's Drew's mother?"

"It would make sense, but go ahead and finish what you were going to say." Christie searched her brain for the first names of Drew's parents, having prepared and delivered quite a few floral arrangements for them the past week. She came up with zilch. All she could remember was "The Simpsons."

"Anyway, Colleen Simpson wants to update the landscaping in the back yard that snugs up to the twelfth green at the club. She said she's heard good things about our work from other clients."

"That's nice to hear. I hope she doesn't change her mind when she sees my face. I delivered flowers to her personally one day last week."

"Do you want me to go to the door alone?" Anita asked warily.

"No," Christie replied. "Running into people who know me from my floral business is an occupational hazard when you live in a small town like White Castle. She just might not realize that I'm doing landscaping as well."

Anita pulled into the spacious driveway in front of the house, which had been built with copper-covered turrets and other features of a French chateau.

"This is quite the house," said Christie. "I'd be tempted to pretend I was Hamlet's Juliet with that balcony over the front entry."

Anita chuckled and said, "That wouldn't surprise me at

all." She led the way with her armload of sketch books and a portfolio of photos of other projects they'd previously done.

Christie took a deep breath and mentally calmed herself while they waited for the door to open.

"I appreciate your promptness," said Colleen. "Please come in for a minute before we go outside to see the area I'd like you to work on." She smiled at Anita and Christie, but her eyes narrowed a moment later as recognition registered.

Addressing Anita, she said, "I didn't realize that Ms. O'Mara was your design partner. I suppose it makes sense, with her beautiful wedding flower business."

Christie smiled and said, "Thank you. This is a beautiful home, Mrs. Simpson. We're thrilled to be invited here." She had to bite her tongue to keep from saying anything about finding dead bodies or skeletons buried in the back yard.

After a few minutes during which Mrs. Simpson named several of her friends who had recommended Prestige Garden Design, their hostess guided them through the house to a pair of enormous French doors that opened onto a flagstone terrace. It was currently laid out as a typical English parterre garden with clipped boxwood hedges around rose beds.

Christie felt certain that neither of the Simpsons were likely to do the maintenance required of such a design. As she half listened to Anita and Colleen talking about changes in the hardscape and general design concepts, her mind wandered. She wondered how much it cost to hire one of the local yard work companies to keep it looking pristine.

"What kind of plants do you think you would suggest for this area in the back?" Anita asked Christie, breaking her reverie. She'd sketched a softer design that eliminated the high-maintenance hedges.

Christie perused the drawing of the new plan. She saw that

Anita had noted the directions of north, south, east, and west on the sketch. That information would guide the selection of specific plants and shrubs, sun-tolerant versus shade-loving, for example, that could accomplish the desired look. Christie added a few notes about the tall trees at the edge of the golf course and other details that could influence her recommendations. "I'm thinking flowering shrubs, low-maintenance perennials and perhaps a centerpiece of a fountain or waterfall with a pond."

"That all sounds lovely," Colleen remarked with a clap of her hands.

Twenty minutes later, they walked around the side of the house toward the entrance after firming up a follow-up visit with Colleen. Christie stopped in her tracks when she saw Drew's BMW pull up into the driveway. He got out, frowned at Anita's SUV, then walked toward the side of the house where Anita and Christie waited, hoping he would go to the front door instead and not see them in the shadows.

"What are you doing here, Ms. O'Mara? I told you to drop it."

Colleen had followed the pair. She looked at her son uncertainly. "Hi, Drew. This is Anita and Christie of Prestige Garden Design. I invited them here to look at the back yard. Do you know them already?"

"Drew probably remembers me from the wedding," said Christie quickly. "Tiffany and her mother had engaged me to do all the flowers."

"Of course," said Colleen. "They were absolutely stunning. Weren't they, Drew?" She looked expectantly at her son. She was still confused about his comment but followed Christie's lead in avoiding more explanation.

Anita grabbed Christie's arm and practically dragged her down the flagstone path toward her rig. "We'll work up a plan and meet with you in a week or two. Thank you for asking us to work on such an exciting project."

Safely in the SUV with windows rolled up and the air conditioner humming, Anita said, "You better talk to McAvoy sooner instead of later."

"I can do it right now." Christie opened her contacts list. "Hey. You just called the detective 'McAvoy' instead of 'Joe.' What gives?"

Anita let out a sigh and smiled sadly. "We had a long talk one day last week about how it's harder to date a well-known person in a small town than it is to be great friends. So we decided that we'd rather remain friends and be able to meet up with you and Jason like we had been instead of officially dating. Does that make sense?" She glanced at her friend. "I mean, with you and Jason, I'm not sure if you're really a couple or simply long-time friends who work well together."

Christie laughed. "I suppose it's something in between those extremes. It helps that we've been friends, including you, since high school. We're just keeping it simple." Her phone buzzed in her pocket. "Speaking of friends, McAvoy is calling right now. I wonder what he wants."

"Hey, McAvoy. What's going on?... You're kidding... I'm with Anita. We'll head that way."

"Where are we going?"

"McAvoy said there's a disturbance at Langley Manor. He'll meet us there and tell us more when we get there."

## CHAPTER
# FORTY-SIX

The gate was wide open when Christie and Anita arrived at Langley Manor. In addition to McAvoy's cruiser, Christie saw three other vehicles in the parking area. "I'm texting McAvoy." *We're here. Now what?*

*Stay there. Newell will meet you.*

*Ok.*

"What's going on?" Anita asked. "What did he say?"

"He's sending Newell to meet us. That's all I know." Christie saw movement on the right side of the house near the former maid's entrance. "There he is now."

Newell hurried to Anita's driver's side window. "Pastor Smith has barricaded himself and Charles Donaldson on the widow's walk. He's threatening to throw Charles down the stairs just like what happened to Debra Ellen."

"Why? What happened?" Christie asked.

"I'm not absolutely sure, but from what the oldest son, Alex, told McAvoy over the phone, they both lied about what happened that night and they're each blaming the other for the young lady's death."

"Why here?" Christie asked.

Newell said, "Come with me. McAvoy is waiting for us inside. He can explain."

Christie and Anita followed Newell into the building, where McAvoy waited in the foyer.

"What's going on?" Christie asked. "Why are you waiting here?"

"Calm down, Christie," said McAvoy.

"What's your plan? Are you going to use a skyhook or something?" Christie asked with her hands on her hips.

"Of course not. We don't have time to get a helicopter here. What I need you to do is go outside and talk to Jeremy from the patio. I figure you have the best relationship with him at the moment. Jeremy has blocked the doorway from the second floor to the third floor. In the meantime, Newell and I are going to go through the maid's quarters and go in the back way. Like you and Anita have done, from what I understand."

"What do you want me to say once I'm out there?"

"Mostly I want you to keep him talking and distracted while Newell and I sneak up the ladder to the widow's walk. Jeremy won't expect us to know about the other entrance. He'll figure he has us locked out."

"What if he has a gun and tries to shoot his way out once he sees you?" Christie asked.

"If that's the case, and it could be, I'll do my best at negotiating with him. I don't want anyone hurt today."

Christie nodded.

"Now, you and Anita get outside and talk to him while we do our part. It should only take a few minutes for us to be in place."

Christie and Anita went through the main door to the patio while the two officers went through the kitchen, then to the patio and around the corner to the back entrance.

Before they were even in sight of the widow's walk, they could hear Jeremy. Christie recognized his voice from their conversations.

"You lied to the police, Mr. Donaldson," Jeremy yelled. "You told me you'd make everything okay if I disappeared."

"But you didn't keep *your* promise, Jeremy. You were supposed to stay away from my family forever." Charles' voice rang out. "Now you'll pay for double-crossing me."

"You know I didn't kill Debra Ellen. You set me up!"

Suddenly, a BMW roared up to the entrance. An attractive man in his forties with gray-tipped black hair hopped out and ran up to Christie and Anita. "I'm Alex Donaldson. What's going on? The police station said I would find the detective here."

Christie explained quickly what had happened while Jeremy and Charles continued to argue and threaten each other.

Alex rushed through the front entrance into the house before Christie could tell him that the stairs had been blocked off.

"He'll figure it out himself in a minute," she muttered. "He knows the house." She glanced at the time. "Come on, Anita. Let's create that distraction. McAvoy and Newell should be in place by now."

Standing below the widow's walk, she whistled. Then she yelled, "Jeremy! It's Christie! What are you doing up there? One of you is going to get hurt. Come on down!" She could see the tops of the two heads above the upper part of the solid rail along the widow's walk. Jeremy was a good several inches taller than the older Mr. Donaldson.

"No way, Christie. I'm not going to let this two-faced liar off this roof alive."

"If you come down, we can talk about it and find out what really happened."

"Not happening. I trusted this man, and he's double-crossed me."

"You can trust *me*, Jeremy," said Christie. "I believe what you told me. Anita's here with me. She believes you too." She realized that neither man was looking down at her. She needed them to look down her way to distract them from what McAvoy planned. But how? The men were concentrating only on each other. She looked at Anita, pointed to a rock on the ground, and mimed throwing it.

Anita nodded, picked up the fist-sized rock from the garden border, and looked to Christie, waiting for a signal to throw it.

All of a sudden, they heard a slam as the door to the widow's walk burst open.

"Alex! What are you doing here? This isn't any of your business," Charles's voice rang out.

"Debra Ellen was my girlfriend, Father, so it *is* my business. I can't let this so-called friend of mine get away with murder."

Jeremy pleaded. "But I didn't kill her. I swear!"

Christie nodded to Anita, who threw the rock with all her strength and hit a metal garbage can next to the kitchen door. At the loud clang, the three men jumped and looked over the edge of the wall, instinctively searching for the cause of the noise.

Then another *clang* rang out as the metal door to the rooftop swung open. The men's heads swung the other way, and the women could now see only the crown of Jeremy's head.

McAvoy's voice rang out. "Stop, all of you. Jeremy, drop the gun. We know it wasn't you."

"No way," said Jeremy. "I knew it was him all along. I saved his ass, and he framed me."

"Officer Newell," said McAvoy, "restrain Mr. Donaldson. Jeremy, drop your gun, or I'll have to charge you as well."

"Yes, Jeremy," said Alex. "I've always believed it was my own father, and now he's going to pay for it."

Christie and Anita heard a single gunshot and a scream.

"Drop the gun, Alex!" McAvoy's voice boomed out. But the women couldn't see anything now, only hear the sounds of the scuffle.

"Call 911!" Christie shouted as she raced into the house and up the steps. She paused only a second at the entry to the widow's walk, fearful of what she would find. Thankfully, she saw that Newell had hand-cuffed Charles Donaldson, who stood with his head bowed. McAvoy was in the process of hand-cuffing Alex, who grumbled, "It wasn't me. I swear it wasn't me!"

Jeremy stood trembling, his face ashen. A small handgun lay on the floor.

"Is anyone hurt? I've called 911," said Christie.

# CHAPTER FORTY-SEVEN

The excitement over for the moment, Christie and Anita drove down to the flower shop. Christie kept thinking how relieved she was that no one had been hurt. Knowing she was supposed to distract the men while McAvoy and Newell surprised them from the other side would only have made her feel all the more responsible if either of the two officers had been hurt in any way.

But it was over. Wasn't it? Something still niggled in her mind and when they arrived, she asked Anita to retrieve the photos from the wedding.

"I want to check out my theory," she said. "Now that we know what Alex Donaldson looks like, we can look at these pictures and see if he's in any of them."

Anita placed them in order of having been taken at the reception.

"Here he is standing next to the pergola with a glass of something," said Christie. "Charles is at that back table with Norma, like Slim pointed out earlier."

"This next picture shows Alex going around the corner,"

said Anita. "Charles is next to the musicians, like he's asking them to play something."

"That corner is where the maid's entrance is behind the hedge," said Christie. "Where is Alex in the next photo?"

"I don't see him at all in the next five pictures, but Charles is in all of them, visiting with guests at different tables."

Christie looked off into space for a moment, then said excitedly, "Hmm. I know what could've happened, Anita."

"What do you mean?"

"Well, we can see Charles in all of these pictures, which suggests he didn't leave the reception and therefore couldn't have been Lauren's killer. But Alex could've gone up the back-stairs, through the maid's quarters, and up to the widow's walk where Lauren was. If she was expecting to meet Charles there, she may have argued with Alex, who showed up instead. I can imagine there was some kind of scuffle, and he tried to shut her up and ended up strangling her and she fell down the stairs."

Anita nodded. "Yes, I can see that."

"Then he went back down through the same route and rejoined the reception in time to be there when Drew and Tiffany announced there had been an incident."

"Which explains why, even though we all suspected Charles, it was his son whom he enlisted to meet with Lauren?"

"Exactly. I'm not sure now why Alex agreed to that, but I'm betting McAvoy can find out once he knows this."

Christie and Anita high-fived each other, then Christie called McAvoy. "Hi, Detective. I believe I've solved your case."

~

Chief Conway gave permission for Christie to sit in on McAvoy's interviews of the two men. She sat on the other side of the two-way mirror, wondering who would be the first man in the metal chair in the other room.

Officer Newell escorted Charles Donaldson into the room, where McAvoy sat waiting, his elbows resting on the table in front of him. Charles was much more subdued than he'd been during his earlier interview a long few days earlier. Newell sat down next to McAvoy.

"Well, Mr. Donaldson. Here we are again. Would you like to tell me what was going on at the manor?"

"Jeremy tricked me into meeting him. He said he had a diary that belonged to someone I know that he wanted to give me."

"And who's that?"

"You don't need to know. Just a friend."

"Does the name 'Cynthia Elliott' ring a bell?"

Christie watched Charles's face register sheer panic. He didn't need to answer the question for her to know his answer.

"Why would Pastor Smith, or Jeremy as you know him, think you might be interested in her diary?"

"I'm sure I don't know," Charles replied. "I don't recognize the name."

McAvoy nodded slowly. "So you don't remember meeting her at Crystal Lake Elementary School and having an affair with her?"

Charles's face reddened. "No, I don't."

"Let's try another question, Mr. Donaldson." McAvoy made a show of opening a file folder in front of him and removing a piece of paper. He turned it around so that Charles could read it. "How is it that a young woman named Lauren Elliott has your DNA? I believe she contacted you recently and may have informed you of your paternal relationship with her."

Charles remained silent. Christie could see the veins of his neck bulging. Drops of sweat dripped down his forehead. He reached for the glass of water on the table.

"Unfortunately, she can't verify that she called you, but your nephew, LeRoy Simpson, is willing to testify that you asked him for money to pay her off. Why would you need to do that?" McAvoy put the DNA results back in the folder.

"I didn't kill her. It was an accident," said Charles.

"Kill who? Debra Ellen? Or Lauren?"

"Neither. It was an accident. I swear."

McAvoy stood. "I'll be back in a moment or two." A few seconds later, he stepped into the room from which Christie and Chief Conway had witnessed the conversation.

He said, "I've got Alex Donaldson in the other room with Officer Newell. He hasn't asked for an attorney yet, maybe because he thinks his arrest is only about shooting the gun at Charles. Fortunately, I hit his arm as he aimed and the bullet went up in the air instead."

"Are you going to tell him what I told you?" Christie asked.

"More or less," said McAvoy. "I also have DNA results that will prove he was on the widow's walk with Lauren."

A few minutes later, the Donaldson men had changed positions. Alex had a smirk on his face as he faced McAvoy, who was sitting with his back to Christie and the chief.

"Would you like to explain to me how your DNA ended up on Lauren Elliott's dress if you haven't ever met her?"

Alex's smirk disappeared for a second. "I haven't the foggiest idea, Detective. You tell me."

"Okay, Mr. Donaldson. Here's what I think happened. You can correct me if I'm wrong."

"Of course, you'll be wrong, but go ahead," said Alex confidently.

"Let's say that your father was being blackmailed by a

young woman named Lauren Elliott. She'd recently discovered through DNA testing that he was her biological father. Through some clever research on her part, she managed to track him down and asked for fifty thousand dollars to be quiet about it, or she would tell his unsuspecting wife."

McAvoy leaned back in his chair. "How am I doing so far?"

"Never heard of her."

"Charles borrowed money from his nephew, your cousin, LeRoy Simpson, to avoid having to explain to his dear wife why he needed fifty thousand dollars. He agreed to meet Ms. Elliott on the widow's walk at his great-nephew's wedding but asked you to go in his place and deliver the money on his behalf."

Alex raised a brow. "That's impossible. I was at the reception with all the other guests while someone else killed her."

McAvoy nodded. "That's partially true, but we know that you left the reception and went up the back stairs to the widow's walk, which explains why none of the waitstaff saw you going upstairs." He tossed a photo on the table.

Alex glanced at it and blanched.

"But one of the photographers caught a picture of you doing exactly that. You had an argument with the young victim, who had hoped to finally meet her father. The two of you struggled, and you strangled her in the process. Then she fell to her death while you returned to the reception without anyone having missed you. But the camera had missed you. You aren't in any more of the following photos, although your father is."

At that moment, Newell entered the room. McAvoy said"Alex Donaldson, you are under arrest for the murder of Lauren Elliott. Read him his rights, please, Office Newell."

## CHAPTER
# FORTY-EIGHT

"The crowd's a lot quieter at the Silver Spoon on Tuesday evenings," said Christie. She was unwinding with Anita and Jason at the local eatery over a pitcher of margaritas and a plate of Mexican tapas.

"Yeah. It feels like ages since we were last here, but I know it's only been a few days," said Anita.

"Which of you is going to fill me in?" Jason asked. "McAvoy gave me a call and said both of you helped resolve the situation at the manor."

Christie and Anita looked at each other and shrugged.

Anita said, "It was mostly Christie. She was diverting the men's attention by telling Jeremy how she believed what he'd told her and that we could work it out if he came down."

Christie said, "It was mostly Anita. She threw a rock at the garbage can and made a racket, which is what really distracted everyone on the widow's walk."

Then Anita said, "But it was Christie who figured out that Alex could've gone up to the widow's walk during the reception and not be missed."

"But it was Anita's photos that proved he was absent."

Jason said, "In other words, good teamwork."

Christie and Anita gave each other one-armed hugs. "Yeah, we're a good team."

McAvoy walked in and joined them at the table, throwing a leg over a backward chair to face them. He sat between Jason and Anita. "I heard that last bit. Yes, you're a good team, all of you."

"Hey, McAvoy!" said Jason. "Good of you to come!"

"Can you have a drink with us? Or are you on duty?" Christie asked when Anita stayed silent.

"With the chief back in town, I am officially off duty until tomorrow at seven a.m., so I'll have one of those margaritas."

Jason poured a glass and handed it to the detective.

"Cheers," he said and raised his glass, then took a swallow.

Christie said to McAvoy, "You're going to fill us in on what Alex told you, right? Who was telling the truth?"

McAvoy took another swallow. "Well, it was something like that story about asking several blind men what an elephant looks like when each of them has only felt one part of the creature. Charles Donaldson, his son Alex, his wife, and Jeremy each told his or her own truth—in other words, what he or she witnessed that evening. It's what they *didn't* say that turned out to be rest of the story, as they say."

"Do tell, Detective," Christie urged. She noticed that Anita stayed silent.

"Okay. What appears to be as close to the truth on that night twenty-five years ago is that Charles is the one who offered to take Debra Ellen home. She told him she needed to tell him something, so they went up on the widow's walk, where she revealed that she was pregnant with his baby. He exploded and told her she had to get an abortion because he couldn't afford to have his reputation as a teacher sullied. She refused and they tussled, and she fell down the stairs. He didn't realize at the time that she was dead, and just went on to the game."

"So, he admitted he was guilty after all?" Christie felt bad that at one point she'd been ready to blame it all on Jeremy.

"Maybe. He swore Debra Ellen was alive when he left and was as surprised as everyone else when they found her dead after the game."

"I'll bet," said Jason. "I wouldn't buy that story if I were in a jury."

"We'll have to wait and see on that," said McAvoy. "Anyway, when Charles and Sarah found Debra Ellen after the game, they saw Jeremy's hat, which could have been there from any of the many times he visited there, who knows? But Charles saw it as an easy out and said that Jeremy must have been there and would have been the last one to see her alive. Later that night, Charles told Jeremy about finding the hat and how it looked to everyone like Jeremy had done it. That's when he told him to leave town to save himself and that he'd cover for him if he did. The three sons weren't questioned rigorously enough at the time. Alex now says that he believed his father was guilty but didn't have any proof. Sarah Donaldson didn't want to believe her husband was guilty, and it was easier to agree with Charles's story."

"But what about Lauren? Where does she fit in all of this?" Christie asked.

"It was Lauren's snooping around that caused Jeremy, now living the life of Pastor Smith, to get worried that she would uncover the lies. He'd become friends with Theresa and Frank Elliott in Elida when he was transferred to their church. Mrs. Elliott shared her concerns about Lauren and her obsession with her mother's death and that Adam had a bad influence on her. That's when Jeremy discovered Adam's blog and the references to Langley Manor. He became even more worried about some kind of discovery."

"But he was innocent," said Christie, "if you believe that Charles was the murderer and the father of Debra Ellen's baby."

"And all this happened twenty-five years ago," said Anita. "Could he still go to jail this many years later?"

Jason interjected. "The district attorney will have to decide but right now, I would venture to guess that Charles will be going to jail for Deba Ellen's death, at the minimum. He might be considered an accessory in Lauren's death as well."

"Anyway," McAvoy continued, "Jeremy learned from Mrs. Elliott that there had been some kind of discovery that led Lauren to believe she'd found her real father through DNA testing. She told Adam that she hoped to meet Charles Donaldson at the wedding when she found out he was Drew's uncle, well, actually great-uncle. She'd already contacted him through one of those DNA-testing sites and threatened to expose him if he didn't give her fifty thousand dollars."

"So that's what Tiffany was talking about at her bachelorette party," said Christie.

"Yes. Adam admitted that Lauren was fully ready to carry out the threat. Charles asked his nephew, LeRoy Simpson—Drew's father—to loan him the money. He didn't want to take that much money out of their retirement account because it would alert his wife that something was going on."

Anita sighed. "I think we can kiss that landscape project at the Simpson house goodbye."

Christie shrugged. "It's okay. There will be others." She and Anita lifted their glasses in a mock toast.

"Did he admit to being 'Skip'?" Christie asked.

"You heard his answer when I mentioned the diary," said McAvoy. "His silence told me what I needed to know."

"Did Alex kill Lauren?" Anita asked quietly.

"He said it was an accident. He said she was surprised when he arrived instead of Charles. When he tried to explain that he had the money but that Charles didn't want to see her, Lauren started screaming that she deserved to see her father, that it wasn't fair to just pay her off like she was nothing, and he tried to cover her mouth. She pulled away and he grabbed her by the skirt of her dress. When he tried to silence her again, his hands slipped down to her neck, and she jerked away and fell down the stairs. Technically speaking, I suppose her death was an accident, but he still caused it."

They were silent around the table for a moment.

"Does Slim know what really happened to Debra Ellen?" Christie asked. "He'll be able to move on now."

"Yes, he knows the truth," McAvoy replied. "Norma Lindemann said she's moving on as well. Two deaths at the hands of her own brother-in-law and nephew is too much for her."

"What will happen to that big orange tabby cat?" Christie asked. "Who's going to take care of him?"

"Now, why don't you all follow me out to the patrol car and then I'll answer your question."

McAvoy opened the passenger door and lifted out a cat carrier.

"It's the ghost cat!" Christie exclaimed. "Are you keeping him, McAvoy?"

"No, I'm not. Slim asked that I deliver him to you, Ms. O'Mara. He thought you would be the best owner. If you'll accept him."

Christie unzipped the opening a few inches and reached a hand into the carrier. The cat meowed loudly, pressed his head against her hand, and began to purr.

"Well, okay, but he needs a name." Christie crossed her arms and placed a finger on her lips. "Hmm. He helped a bit in solving the murder, a little like Sherlock Holmes's friend. I'm going to name him 'Watson.' "

THE END

# ACKNOWLEDGMENTS

As always, I must compliment my amazing editor, Sandra Herner. I swear she's clairvoyant! She can take anything I've written and make suggestions that improve my story. Thank you!

My friend Marcia planted the seed about the mansion and met with Mrs. Robinson and I to learn more about the history of the beautiful home. Thank you!

My friend Angela encouraged me when I was discouraged, and read through several iterations of many chapters. She has the patience of Job. Thank you!

And, I thank my copy editor, Donna West, for her diligence in finding all those extra commas and apostrophes that tend to sprinkle through the pages. Thank you!

# About the Author

PJ Peterson is an emerging author of both cozy mysteries and amateur sleuth mysteries. This is the fourth book in her Christie's Flower Shoppe cozy mysteries series.

She has added two kitties to her family in the past year. Buttons, a silky black female who looks like Stormy from the covers, was an abandoned 2 day-old kitten when found. She is daring and sleek, as well as lovable and defiant. Cheddar, a ginger tabby male, had been rescued from a home with too many animals and nursed back to health by the same young family who raised Buttons. He is the purr-ingest, loving-est, gentlest cat I've ever met. I had to write him into the story lest he be jealous about his "sibling's" fame.

She has written seven Julia Fairchild mysteries as well, and is considering writing another one in the near future. Her friends love to feed her story ideas.

The books are all available on Amazon, with some of them in audiobook form as well.

www.ingramcontent.com/pod-product-compliance
Lightning Source LLC
LaVergne TN
LVHW091123080826
845145LV00008B/2026